SALVATION

BLACK HOODS MC#7

TRIGGER WARNINGS

This book contains graphic scenes of violence, sexual assault, death, kidnapping, drug use, human trafficking, and sexual encounters.

Dark Salvation

Priest just woke up in hell. Hell is Boo's reality.

When Priest leaves the Sturgis Motorcycle Rally, he didn't know his life was about to change. Run off the road, held captive and beaten, he finds himself in the middle of a war. His captors want him to betray his club, but that will never happen. And who is the woman sneaking into his cell? She's beautiful, broken and full of fear. Priest knows he has to escape, but can he leave her behind?

Boo has never known life away from the Screwballs MC. She was just a child when they bought her, making her a slave for their own sick pleasures. She has always done whatever she needed to survive. She's a prisoner without a cell, and she's accepted that as her fate. But then the stranger shows up, bloodied and tortured and locked in the cell. He's different from these men. He shows her genuine kindness and concern. He also wants her to help him escape, but can she trust him?

Each of them has to make a choice. Do they save the other or save themselves?

To Deadlines.
We Still Fucking Hate You.
Avelyn & Geri

Chapter 1

PRIEST

"STOP RIDING my ass and go around, fucker," I growl, gesturing for the truck behind me to pass.

I've been on this road for close to an hour, and being so early in the morning, there's been little to no traffic. And then, this asshole comes out of nowhere, flying up on my ass. After nearly three miles, it appears they're intent on staying there.

The road ahead is clear, stretching on for miles into the grasslands, with the sun breaking out above the distant mountains. The scenery of Oklahoma's Wichita Mountains' foothills is breathtaking, and exactly what I'd been looking forward to when I set out early this morning. I'd been enjoying it too, before this fucking truck appeared.

Waving my arm like a lunatic now, I yell, "Go around!"

My body tenses when the driver ignores my directive and inches closer. People don't normally tailgate a motorcycle, especially when its rider is wearing a patch for a well-known motorcycle club. People avoid MC members, not wanting to risk getting on their bad side. But clearly, this fucker is lacking common sense.

I accelerate, watching in the side mirror as the driver speeds up, determined to stay close. Just when I think shit can't get any worse, I see a van barreling up behind us, eating up the pavement.

My stomach drops to my ass as I take in my situation. A lone rider on an empty highway at seven o'clock in the morning, with no other members of my club at my back. A very stupid move, now that I think about it.

The general rule of thumb with the Black Hoods MC is that no man rides alone. We always pair up, because there's safety in numbers. Granted, I *was* paired up, until TK found his soulmate in Sturgis and decided to stay behind, just as we were ready to head out. So here I am, without backup, on a lonely stretch of highway. Things are about to get real nasty.

The van is closer now, approaching fast, while the truck creeps up, coming within inches of my rear fender. I push my motorcycle as fast as it'll go, but the driver matches my speed, and the van increases theirs until they're directly behind the truck.

We're moving at a dangerous speed. Every crack and

pebble on the paved road beneath me feels like a boulder meant to throw me off course. The effort it's taking to keep both wheels on the ground has my heart pounding like an angry drum against my chest.

Please, God. Help me make it out of this alive.

My relationship with God has been tested over the past few years—strained, to say the least—but I believe He is up there, listening, and that He is with me now, no matter the outcome.

The van pulls out from behind the truck and again speeds up.

Fuck. Fuck. Fuck.

Then the van is beside me. I'm trapped, and there's nothing I can do. The shoulder of the road butts up to an endless expanse of short brown grass and pebbled soil, sure to tear me to shreds should I maneuver in that direction. And I can't go any faster than I am right now. I have the throttle twisted to the max, and I still can't pull ahead.

Fear and anger twist inside my gut, burning me up from the inside out. Why did I put my gun in the saddlebag instead of on my belt like I usually do?

I was foolish.

Making my way back to Texas, I'd been taking my time, hungry for the open road to cleanse my soul and clear my mind. I'd forgotten who I am, though. I'm not just some asshole on a motorcycle. I'm a member of the

Black Hoods MC, and driving anywhere unarmed is fucking stupid. *I'm* fucking stupid.

Turning my head, just slightly, while fighting to keep the motorcycle steady, I gaze over at the van. The passenger, with an evil grin on his ugly face, is Big Dick, president of the Screwballs MC. In any other instance, I would laugh at the bruises still marring his face from the ass-kicking he had gotten from my brother, TK. But this was not the time nor place, sadly.

Fuck.

I dart my eyes to the road ahead before turning back to glare at Big Dick, sure the asshole is going to shoot me any moment.

His eyes never leaving mine, he shouts, "Now!"

The van veers right. The side mirror narrowly misses my head as it smashes into me, crushing my leg between it and my ride. At the same time, the truck hits me from behind, and then I'm flying. My brain barely has enough time to register how bad this is going to fucking hurt before I hit the hard earth and skid across the grass.

My world immediately goes black.

Chapter 2

BOO

"MISSED A SPOT," Tammy chirps, knocking over the sudsy bucket next to me with her foot. "Oops!" Giggling, she sways her hips as she approaches the club members watching something on the big screen TV hanging over the bar. Sauntering past several of the guys, one grabs her arm and tugs her into his lap. She squeals happily and settles into his embrace, like the good little girl she pretends to be when they're watching.

Why she's desperate for their attention is beyond me, but I get it. When you make them happy, shit's not as hard around here. The guys go a little easier on the amiable, pliable ones who open their legs, or mouth, whenever they get their cocks out, like baby birds starving for their cum. All pathetic attempts at adapting to our shitty situation and making the best of it. Something that I will never do. Do I get fucked just like the rest of them? Of course I do. They own me, lock, stock, and barrel, but that doesn't mean I enjoy what they do to my body. I find absolutely no pleasure in their touch.

Alan, the Screwballs MC treasurer, instantly takes notice of the mess and sneers, shaking his head in disapproval. "Fucking clean it up, Boo."

"Yes, sir." Pushing up off my knees, I stalk off toward the utility closet, grab a stack of the newly washed towels I'd just put away, and head back to the mess where I toss them to the floor. Not only do I have to take care of this, but now I have more laundry to do later.

Fucking Tammy.

It always has to be her. She's made my already miserable life fucking hell since the day she showed up with one of the guys, begging for sanctuary. First, her story was that she was running from an abusive ex, to then being on the run from some asshole she owed money to. Whatever the truth was, she stayed and never left. Granted, I'd been here longer than any of the girls on constant rotation in and out of the clubhouse. But for her, it had been a considerable amount longer than most. Between her and Alan, I'm not sure who's worse: the bitch who causes me so much trouble, or the son of a bitch who claims my body for himself every night.

Alan's dark gaze watches me as I clean up the soapy

water. One of the newer prospects shifts off his barstool near the front door to come to my aid, but Alan growls out menacingly, "Stay away from her." The prospect raises his hands up and parks his ass back on his perch, Alan's warning clear.

I'm his toy. No other man gets to touch me.

Alan smirks, clearly satisfied with the prospect's response, until he sees me watching the exchange. He's off his stool in a flash, stomping toward me in his heavy boots. Before I can attempt to get away, he's on me, his large hand snatching one of my hot pink braids and yanking me to him.

"You're mine," he snarls next to my ear. To the room, he declares, "You hear me? This bitch is fucking mine!" The room responds in muffled acknowledgements.

Before I can stop myself, I spit, "I'm not yours." The second the words leave my mouth, his free hand wraps around my throat, applying enough pressure to restrict my airway. I thrust my hands at his chest, trying to push him away with all my might, but Alan has at least a hundred pounds on me. Even in a fair fight, my buck forty frame is no match for him.

"When is my little mouse gonna learn? That pretty little cunt won't keep saving you from that smart mouth of yours, no matter how much I like it wrapped around my cock."

I try again to fight back, but he adjusts his grip and squeezes. Black spots pop up in my vision, as I feel my body growing slack from the pressure he's applying.

"Say you're mine," he demands.

"No," I rasp out.

"Say it, bitch." Again, he tightens his grip. "Right here, in front of everyone."

"Dude," one guy calls out from behind him. "Bitch's lips are turning fucking blue. You're killing her." His voice carries no sense of urgency to help, nor any concern. Just stating a fact. "You know Prez won't like it if you kill another one of the girls."

Another one? I knew Alan was a twisted fuck of a man, but the knowledge that I'm not the first girl he's handled like this rocks me to my core. Was she like me? Did she fight back? Was she sold to their club too, to pay off someone's debt?

Alan loosens his hold, snapping me back to my bleak reality, and warns, "He won't save you, Boo. Say it, and I'll let you go."

The fight has completely left me, so I gasp out, my voice hoarse, "Yours."

"Good girl."

As soon as he releases me, I fall onto my knees, gasping for air, the headache now thrumming through my ears, beating in tandem with my heart. It takes a few minutes for my breathing to even out and for my vision to clear. Minutes that are my only reprieve from Alan's attention. Taking a deep breath and blowing it out slowly, I go to stand up, but Alan grabs my shoulders and pushes me back down.

"Time to show them who you belong to, Boo." Fumbling with his belt, he unzips his pants and pulls out his flaccid cock, ordering me to, "Suck it."

My stomach churns at the demand. One he's given me more times than I care to admit since my uncle sold me to this club. The very first time he sought me out, the night of my eighteenth birthday, and the eighth year of belonging to the Screwballs. He fucked me right on the pool table in the middle of a game, only stopping to take his turn with the cue. He left me there all night once he was finished, tied down to the table, and left for anyone who wanted a turn. They all did. After that night, Alan kept me to himself, or so he thought. If he only knew his club president and vice president had taken their own liberties with my body while he was out on errands. I seriously doubt he'd take that news well.

Steeling myself against what I'm about to do, I lean forward and open my mouth.

"That's right. Show them who those lips belong to. Show them you're mine."

I wrap my lips around his soft cock and suck, all

while trying to drown out the actions with the noises around the room, and counting down the seconds with Mississippi's like I'd learned from watching the kiddie educational videos they used to plop me down in front of instead of going to school.

One Mississippi. Two Mississippi. Three…

A loud crash reverberates from the front door as Big Dick, the club president, kicks it open with force. Alan shoves me away, quickly tucking his dick back into his pants.

"Brought us a present, boys." Beaming, Big Dick shoves a man inside and onto the floor.

I try to get a good look at him, but he's a real mess. His long hair is caked in blood, obscuring his face completely. He rasps out unintelligible moans, which gets him a hard kick to the ribs from Big Dick.

"Take him to the cells," he orders.

Two men grab the injured man by his arms and drag him toward the cells located in the back room. I shift my gaze as they pass me, and notice he's wearing a vest like the Screwballs, but with a different logo and colors. *He's in an MC.* Alan catches me watching as they pass, so I avert my gaze, but not before I see the words written on the back of his vest as he disappears around the corner.

Black Hoods MC.

Was that the club Big Dick had been raging on about

since they came back from Sturgis? The one who had his kid and beat his ass six ways from Sunday? That's something I would have loved to see in person. At least someone is standing up to them. And if this man is a member, could he possibly be my one shot out of here?

Chapter 3

PRIEST

COLD WATER SPLASHES OVER ME, tearing me out of the darkness and plunging me back into the land of the living.

"Rise and shine, asshole," a voice cackles from somewhere nearby.

I glance around the room, my head swimming with pain and confusion. *Where am I? What happened?*

A tall figure steps into my field of vision, and my heart sinks like a stone. Big Dick. *The van. I crashed. I died.*

But I didn't die. I'm here, so I definitely didn't die. But where is here? And why the fuck are my arms chained to the ceiling?

Rage envelops me as I struggle against my bonds, but they've made escape impossible. My wrists are bound together with rope and chains, and tethered to a beam in the ceiling. My ankles are restrained in the same way, but bolted to the floor.

I roar in frustration, my scream so loud, I fear my throat will disintegrate in its wake.

Laughter surrounds me. So many men. There are at least ten of them standing in the shadows of the room, but not deep enough that I can't commit their faces to memory. The white lettering of their Screwballs MC patch nearly glows in the dark, and my gut twists as I realize just how truly fucked I am.

These assholes aren't playing around. They don't care that their actions will start a war with the Black Hoods. They're not intending to let me go.

"Untie me," I snarl, wishing I could blow Big Dick's head off with my glare alone.

Big Dick's lips part in an evil grin. "You were right, Nutsy," he calls out to one of the other men in the room. "Fucker does look like Jesus." He turns his attention back to me and takes a step closer. "That why they call you Priest, asshole?"

"Untie me," I repeat through gritted teeth, using the leverage of my bindings to lean toward him. Big Dick is a big motherfucker, but at six foot eight, I'm bigger. He and I both know I could snap him like a fucking twig if given the chance. "Untie me and find out, fuckface."

Chuckling, Big Dick says, "That's not gonna happen." His words are slightly mispronounced, thanks to the fat, bruised lip he'd received from TK back in Sturgis. "We need to have a chat," he continues. "You fucked up big time when you intervened in my family business. So now, you're gonna make it up to me by giving me some information, and helping me get my son from his bitch mother."

Anger brews inside of me like an inferno. Big Dick had raped my friend Cora. And the "son" he's talking about is little Harrison, the result of that rape. He's too young to understand where he came from, but Cora's been raising that boy with love and patience. Something he would never get from the monster in front of me.

"I'm not telling you shit."

His fist slams into my nose before I even process his movement, knocking my head back, and causing my entire body to swing from my binds. It's broken; I heard the pop. And if that weren't enough, I can feel the blood pouring down my face and the back of my throat.

"Wrong answer, preacher boy."

My eyes are watering so badly, I can barely make out his blurred shape as he walks in circles around me.

"You have no idea who you're fucking with, do ya, asshole? You might think you and your club are tough shit, but we're the real fucking deal. The one-percenters. The ones who will kill you where you stand, and leave your bodies in a pile for the police to find later. We don't care about laws and public image. We run our own little corner of the world, and now, you're in it. I'm the fucking law around here."

His hand darts out and grabs something on my cut. I look down, rage brewing through my pain as he flicks a knife through the threads holding the one-percenter patch to my chest.

"You stupid fucks don't deserve this patch."

Lifting my gaze from the loose threads surrounding the now empty space on my cut, I look down at Big Dick. "You just signed your death notice."

Big Dick pauses, one brow raised as he smirks. "That so? You gonna kill me from your chains, preacher boy?"

I hold his glare, my rage ratcheting up and turning into something I've never felt before. A need for destruction. A need to see this man's life bleed into the earth while his soul is sucked into the fiery pits of Hell, where he'll spend his eternity. And I'll be right behind him, ready to make him suffer more than Satan ever could.

Something passes over his face as I stare at him, like a flicker of fear, but he squashes it before it has a chance to settle into place. His fist rockets into my gut, stealing the air from my lungs before I can blink.

My lungs heave, struggling to pull in oxygen. But instead, they seem frozen in my chest from the impact of his blow.

"I know Cora left town with that long-haired fucker, and she took my boy with her. Where did they go?"

I can't breathe. My lungs are useless, unable to function as I hang in place from my chains.

Big Dick steps forward again, a knife now in his hand. "Where did they go?" he roars through gritted teeth.

I hold his hate-filled stare, the tiniest bit of oxygen filling my lungs. Just enough to keep me from passing out. Big Dick presses the tip of the knife to my belly. "Where. Did. They. Go?"

I'm still sucking in air, but only the smallest bit is going into my lungs. My head swims, and I know I'm about to pass out. My stomach rolls, ready to release its contents all over the floor in front of me.

Big Dick's face is in mine, the blade still pressed into my stomach. Enough that I can feel the tip of it break my skin through my shirt

"Where did they go?" he roars, his eyes wild.

I open my mouth as if to answer, and when Big Dick presses closer, ready to hear what I have to say, I gather up the saliva in my mouth and spit it directly into his face.

Big Dick blinks at me in shock, his expression turning to disgust, and the knife at my gut disappears. The next thing I see is him slamming his head forward and into my already pulverized nose.

Darkness takes over. A sweet escape, no matter how brief.

Chapter 4

BOO

SNEAKING from Alan's bed in the middle of the night, risking his ire later for leaving him when he'd ordered me to stay, I find my way back to the small room I share with two other girls, only to find my small pallet in the corner occupied by someone else. *Just my luck.* With a defeated shrug, I head down to the shared bathroom. At least with everyone asleep, I can enjoy the hot water in peace before everyone else uses it up.

Reaching inside the dingy, mint green tile stall, I twist the knob. The water pressure sputters until a steady stream finally appears. For a club with so much dirty money, between the drugs they peddle and the women they traffic, you'd think they could at least afford some upgrades to their clubhouse. Guess their money is best spent elsewhere.

I return to the row of sinks and peer into the mirror,

taking in the thick dark circles under my eyes. Sleep never comes easily anymore. I never know when to expect Alan to want me to service him, or someone else wanting me for chores. The only time I ever seem to sleep is when Alan chokes me out, or I'm lucky enough to conk out from sheer exhaustion.

What a life I live now.

I draw my hand up to my cheek, delicately fingering the bruise forming from my time with Alan last night. A mirror image to the finger shaped bruises he'd left on my throat. My light freckled skin shows every mark and scar. Even my hazel eyes are dim under the torturous care of the Screwballs MC. My hair is askew, with little pink stray pieces sticking out from my braids. The rosy hue has faded without proper care or more hair dye. I was lucky to get some as it was. I'd found it cleaning out the room of one of the girl's they'd sold, hidden away in her suitcase. I'd always wanted to see what I would look like with pink hair, so I tried it. My reward for doing something for myself? A black eye from Alan, because he hated it.

You're a mess, Boo. A goddamn mess.

I grip the edges of the sink as hot tears spill from my eyes. Crying seems to be my only outlet to the life I've been dealt, and only in these quiet moments to myself do I allow them to rise to the surface and break free. I cry for the pain inflicted upon my body. I cry from the frustration of not being able to change my situation, because I know, deep down, the only way I'll get out of here is in a body bag, or buried in some hole with God knows how many other countless, nameless women this club has chewed up and spit out. Shells of their former selves because of their own, or someone else's mistake, of crossing this club.

I allow myself to sob until there's nothing left. No more tears. No more energy.

Stripping down, I step into the shower and let the hot water soak into my cold soul. Back against the wall, I slide down till my bottom hits the floor, wrap my arms around my knees, and allow my mind to drift to things outside of this hellhole that could help me find some peace. I eventually start to doze off under the spray, finding some sort of quiet comfort, until someone jerks back the curtain, allowing cold air to seep into my warm sanctuary.

"There you are," Tammy purrs, her devious smile almost cat-like on her round face, her red hair twisted up in a messy bun. I'd almost say she was pretty if I didn't know she had a soul as black as the men in this club. Tammy wasn't like the rest of us, because unlike us, she wanted to be here. "Look at you, pathetic little Boo, trying to hide from her fate."

"What do you want, Tammy?" I murmur, shifting my gaze back to the tops of my knees.

"Alan's looking for you."

He never leaves me alone. He's like my unwanted shadow, following me wherever I go, no matter how small of a space we're in. If it hadn't been for the extra whiskeys he'd had last night, celebrating with the club over their new prisoner, I doubt I'd have been able to find my reprieve this morning. He was stone-cold passed out when I left his room.

"Why did he send you if he's looking for me? He stalks me just fine on his own."

"It's cute how you try to fight back, Boo. Watching that smart mouth of yours pissing off Alan is one of my favorite pastimes around here. Keep it up, will you? Your defiance makes me look good."

"Sure thing," I mumble, rolling of my eyes. "Anything to make it easier on you, Tammy." If I knew how to make it harder for her, I'd do it in a heartbeat. She deserves all the bad shit for what she deals out to the other girls tenfold. Jozie, the girl who had come in shortly after me, died after Tammy spiked her cocktail with enough roofies to tranquilize a full-grown horse, all because she wanted her to stop crying so Tammy could get some sleep. Thanks to her, the guys put a stop to us drinking, taking away the one thing we had to numb ourselves with. Of course, Tammy spun it, making it out as if she committed suicide. And with a few rounds of blow jobs, the club was inclined to believe her. *Idiots*.

"That's a good girl." She starts to walk away, but then stops, peering over her shoulder with a sinister smile. "Better hurry. You don't want to keep Alan waiting."

I'd keep him waiting for the rest of my life if I could.

Getting to my feet, I turn off the water, step out of the stall, and wrap myself up in a towel. The abrupt change in temperature sends goosebumps along my exposed skin. I quickly gather my discarded clothes and rush back to my room. Depositing my dirty clothes on my now empty bed, I throw on some clean underwear, a fresh pair of jeans, and a plain white T-shirt.

Running a comb through my pink hair, I coil it into a tight bun at the base of my neck and head out to the main room, where it's quiet this time of day. Early mornings aren't exactly popular for a bunch of guys whose work is often done under the cloak of darkness. A few of the other girls shuffle in and out of the galley-style kitchen behind the bar, each of them carrying a small bowl. Cherry, another one of the imprisoned girls, spots me and waves me over. I want to join them, but I know the consequences of making Alan wait.

With a smile, I shake my head and make my way toward Alan's room in the officer's hallway, my heart racing with each step I take. I knew sneaking out would piss him off, and the fear of what lies behind that door scares the hell out of me. Would he chain me up this time? Whip me like he had a few weeks ago when I dared to go outside for some fresh air after the club had filleted a man in the middle of the main room? That had also earned me a shiny new ankle monitor, linked straight to Alan's phone. If I stepped out of the club-house, he'd be on me in a flash. With Alan, it's a toss of which version of Hyde I'll be greeted with. There is no Jekyll side to him. Just a monster in a leather vest.

I suck in a breath, trying to steel myself for whatever lies ahead of me, then exhale before knocking on the door.

"Get in here, Boo," Alan growls from the other side of the door.

My hand trembles as I turn the handle. Slowly, I push open the door and step inside, finding Alan sitting on the edge of his bed, his hair still askew from last night. One of his kinks is having me pull it while he does as he pleases with my body. It's a small sacrifice to make if it ends my torment quicker.

Not looking at me, he demands, "Where were you?"

"I took a shower." My voice wavers with each sylla-ble. "I didn't want to wake you up, so I used our shower. I must have fallen asleep. I meant to come back to your room after." The lie rolls off my tongue far easier than it should. Alan's piercing gaze shifts over to me, as if he's analyzing my body language to determine if I'm telling the truth. "I was alone," I add. "Ask Tammy. She found me there."

"I shouldn't have to ask someone else to track you down." With a hard shove, he's on his feet, his naked body on full display, the thick hair on his chest matted from sweat. A deep frown forms on his face as he cups his large hand over the bruise on my cheek. "I wouldn't have to hurt you if you'd just fucking listen."

"I know," I murmur, casting my eyes down to avoid his. "I'm sorry."

The words feel like acid on my tongue, because I'm not sorry. The only person I should be apologizing to is myself, for allowing this to happen. For not seeing the debt my uncle was collecting at an alarming rate, and not seeing his intent to use me to pay it until it was too late.

"I went easy on you this time, but if you don't start behaving, Boo, I won't be able to control my temper." Caressing my cheek, he places a kiss there. It takes everything in me to keep from recoiling from his touch. It's like millions of stinging fire ants crawling all over my skin when he touches me. "You know what happens when I get pissed off."

The scars on my back from his whip are proof enough that I know that answer. Torture of a different kind. It's one thing to fuck my unwilling body, but it's another to cut into it, leaving marks I'll have to live with for the rest of my life, however long that may be.

"Try to behave today, won't you? Big Dick is on edge with our new guest."

"I understand."

"Good girl." Releasing me, he steps away and starts getting dressed. Once he's finished, he grabs me by the arm and drags me back out into the main room. I dutifully follow along until he deposits me outside of the kitchen and disappears inside. When he returns a few minutes later, he hands me a plate of mush.

"Come with me." Grabbing hold of me again, he leads me down the opposite hallway, toward the cells. My stomach lodges in my throat. Is he putting me back into the cells? Is this my punishment? How did taking a shower regulate me to this?

Alan doesn't stop until we reach the heavy outer door. He releases me long enough to jerk it open. It hits the wall so hard, it makes me jump. Once open, he grabs me again and yanks me inside.

My skin crawls at the memory of my time here. My first three years with the Screwballs, this was my home. I'd only been taken out to get cleaned up or to clean the clubhouse. I was ten years old. Far too young to be a plaything like the other girls. Big Dick had said my cell was for my own protection, but in reality, it was to keep me under lock and key until they broke me and made me compliant. Only then was I allowed free rein inside the main areas of the clubhouse. The only freedom I'd ever been given.

We stop outside an occupied cell. On the other side of

the bars, a figure lies on a tattered cot, curled into themselves in a protective cocoon against the damp cold. The
familiar sight of dark, matted hair is the only way I
recognize him. It's the man from the Black Hoods they
had brought in last night from God knows where.

"What am I doing here?" I whisper.

"You'll see." His words set off warning signals inside
my head, and my heart nearly stops. He's really going to
lock me up here, again, over a fucking shower.

"Alan, I didn't mean to piss you off," I start, but he
hushes me.

"Enough, Boo. Just watch."

Pulling down a small flap, he takes the plate from my
hand and pushes it through, onto the floor.

The man on the cot never moves. "You're to feed him
once a day," Alan orders. "Only that. In and out. You got
it? Don't speak to him."

"Wait, what?" I'm confused. Why are they trusting
me with this task? Surely this responsibility is better
suited for someone like Tammy. Someone who wants to
please the club.

"Don't make me repeat myself, Boo. You know how
much that irritates me."

"Yes, sir," I submit. "Once a day. Don't talk to him."

"Good girl."

"Who is he?"

"None of your concern. You just make sure he has a meal each morning."

With a jerk, Alan tugs me behind him, leaving the man alone in the cells once more. He brings me back to the main room and releases me before stalking off to join a few other Screwballs at the table. Cherry slides over the bowl she'd made for me as I take my spot with the women. They chatter away, but my mind is a million miles away.

The men talk in hushed tones, and I strain to listen to their conversation. Big Dick's voice rises just enough for me to make out the words "ransom" and "son".

Shit, I was right. This man belongs to the club that has his son. Alan may have just handed me a gift with my new task. Feeding the one person who may have enough friends to help get him out. And if I play this right, maybe he can save me.

Chapter 5

PRIEST

MY BRAIN THROBS. It feels like a marching band of bass drummers are having drum line practice inside my skull. The thin strip of light from the window above me does little to illuminate the dark, damp room. All I can make out are the four cement walls encasing me. A makeshift bed creaks underneath as I try to move.

"Fuck," I groan. Every muscle in my body screams in agony with any movement I make. It's been days, I think, since I was brought here, maybe longer. Endless cycles of darkness and brief periods of consciousness has my mind all messed up.

My stomach growls. Turning as far as I can on the bed, I retch over the side.

I lie here in pain for what feels like hours before a clunking noise draws my attention to the metal door. I stay quiet as a woman with hot pink braids on either side of her face slips inside the room, then quietly closes the door behind her.

"I brought you something to eat." Taking a few steps forward, she reveals a paper plate with a slice of bread and a smear of peanut butter across it. I try shifting in the cot, but my body is weak.

My hands shake as I bring the bread to my lips. It stings when I swallow, feeling like sandpaper against my throat. I have to cough in an attempt to force it down.

"I'll bring you water next time. They were watching me. I couldn't bring both."

"Where am I?"

"I can't tell you. If they knew I was in here, they'd kill me."

My mind is so cloudy, I can barely think straight.

I study her pale face, taking in the scars that mark her cheeks and trail down to her collarbone and shoulders. Her left eye is black and blue from a fresh strike that could only be a few days old.

"What do they want with me?"

"I don't know that, either."

"Then why are you helping me?"

"Because the only way to survive here is giving them what they want, and the only way we're getting out of here is if you're still alive."

I pause with the bread at my lips. "Who are you?"

"My name is Boo." She points to the patch on my chest. "Priest?"

Nodding, I take another bite. This girl looks beaten and broken beyond repair, except for her eyes. They're sad, but there's life in them… hope.

"I heard them talking," she whispers, her words coming out in a rush. "I couldn't hear what they said, but they were talking about Big Dick's son, and something about a ransom."

That fucker is relentless. He's been beaten and blocked from getting to that boy at every turn, and yet, he keeps trying. His mother would never allow him to get near him. And even if he managed to get past her, little Harrison has the entire Black Hoods MC at his back, ready to put their lives on the line to keep him from his disgusting sperm donor.

"You need to get me out of here," I say, sitting up a little straighter.

Shaking her head sadly, Boo points to a thick black box banded to her ankle. "I can't even get myself out of here."

Anger, defeat, hopelessness, and despair wash over me like a tidal wave. I'm never getting out of this cell. Not alive, anyway. I have no say in the matter, but I do have a say in what to do with my time here. They think they can break me and get me to give them Harrison? I'll die before I tell them anything.

Just then, footsteps echo down the hallway, and Boo's eyes fill with terror as someone approaches.

"You stupid bitch," a tall, older man growls as he storms into view. "What do you think you're doing? I told you to feed him and leave. What were you saying to him?"

"Nothing," Boo splutters, her body trembling. "He asked for water, and I was just telling him that I hadn't brought any."

The man's hand comes out and connects with her face, his rings cutting her lip with the impact. Boo falls back a step, but keeps her footing.

"I'm sorry, sir. It won't happen again."

The man's eyes move from her to me, but I'm too weak to stand, let alone rip him limb from limb like I wish I could.

"You don't fucking talk to her, asshole. You hear me? She's mine. Everybody knows it, and now you do too. Say one word to her, I'll kill you myself."

And with that, he grabs one of Boo's braids and drags her away, slamming the door at the end of the hall behind them. The lock thunks back into place, and as their footsteps disappear, I can still hear the rage in his voice as he screams at her.

Chapter 6

BOO

"WERE YOU TALKING TO HIM?" Alan bellows as he strikes me across the face, the impact of his blow knocking me off balance. I stagger, hitting the wall behind me with a thud. By sheer instinct alone, I wrap my arms around my face to protect myself from him. The action only pisses him off more. "Answer me!"

"No, I didn't talk to him! I just told him I didn't bring water." I lie, like it's the last one I'll ever tell. Truthfully, it might be if Alan doesn't believe me, because I'm dead if he doesn't. That's a sure-fire fact. "I was doing what you told me to do!"

"I told you to feed him and leave. Why were you still in there?"

"He scared me," I whimper. "I was putting his bowl on the floor, like you showed me, and he moved. I didn't know what to do." *Lie. Lie. Lie.*

Alan's large frame presses against me as he pulls my arms from around my head. His large fingers pinch my chin, dragging my gaze up to his. "I'm only going to ask this one more time, Boo. Did you talk to him?"

"No!" I cry out.

With a huff, Alan releases my chin. He doesn't move, though, putting no distance between us. He stares down at me, his dark irises almost inking out the whites of his eyes. Alan's been angry with me before, but never like this. What is it about the prisoner that has him and his entire club on edge? Ever since he arrived, there's been an off feeling in the air that has replaced their initial excitement about his capture.

"If I catch you in there alone like that again, Boo, you know what'll happen. If he tries to talk to you or touch you, you leave and come find me." His shoulders square, his anger wafting out through every pore. Was that it? Did he think he touched me? Touched what was his?

"Yes, sir," I whisper.

"Good girl." He tamps down his anger and smiles. I almost gag. "Always my good little mouse. So eager to please."

Bile rises up my throat, but I swallow it down the best I can. If Alan knew how I really felt about him, things would be so much worse for me. Giving him the upper hand is the only way I survive here. The more he trusts me to follow his strict orders, the better chance I have of being left alone with the prisoner again. Today was by sheer chance. I'm going to need a fucking miracle for it to happen again. All I can do is play my part and hope for the best that I get that chance again.

Priest can help me. I know he can. He's my only hope.

Hope. The word makes me laugh. I've put so much stock into that word since I got here. Hope that my uncle would pay off his debts and let me come home. Hope that Alan gets killed on a run and never comes back. Hope that I make it out of this hellhole alive.

Hope is a thing for those who wish for change, and have no means of actually achieving it. A feeble ideal that our mind clings to when nothing makes sense in the world. Here, hope gets you killed, or sold to the highest bidder. No, I can't hope for the best. I have to grab it by the fucking balls and make it happen, even if playing along kills another piece of my soul every day I'm under this roof.

"I'm sorry for making you mad. I didn't mean to make you angry with me."

"How sorry are you?"

"Very," I reply, trying not to choke on the word.

Alan's hands roam down my body, going lower, until one digs in between my legs. "Is this cunt of yours wet for me? Does it ache for my touch?"

"Yes," I hiss. I have to choke back tears as the lie

passes through my lips. Thick waves of nausea roll through my insides like a swirling sea.

Play your part, Boo. Play it.

"Show me how sorry you are, then."

It takes everything I have not to recoil when my hands fumble with his belt. My fingers tremble slightly when I go to pull down his zipper, feeling his cock already hard against it. Beating me did this. My screams and tears did this.

I hesitate, and Alan notices.

"Get it out," he orders. "You want my forgiveness? Earn it."

With a nod, I sink to my knees. Offering my mouth is a lesser evil than giving him my body. The disgust I feel for myself grows with each passing second.

Alan grabs the back of my head and forces me closer to him. His fingers dig into my scalp, and a tear slips down my stinging cheek before I can stop it.

"Fuck, I love it when you cry. Makes the blowjob so fucking good."

I steel myself against what I'm about to do, but I'm saved momentarily by someone knocking at Alan's door.

"Fuck off!" he yells. "I'm busy."

"Big Dick wants you," a voice calls from the other side of the door. "Says it's important."

Alan roars, his face twisted in anger. "Can't it wait five fucking minutes?"

"It's about the prisoner. Got some new information out of him. Prez called church."

"Fuck!" Shoving me to the floor, he tucks himself back into his jeans and throws open the door. The dark-haired prospect who tried to help me with the bucket incident stands on the other side, his fist raised as if he was about to knock again. Peering past Alan, the prospect scowls when he sees me on the floor.

"Do you have to rough her up so much?" he asks.

"She's mine to do what I fucking want with, and you'd do well to remember that, prospect. I should kill you just for looking at her."

The prospect takes a step back from his spot, his hands raised in surrender. Standing up to Alan will have him out of the club in a heartbeat, and he knows that. Hell, I know that. He'd lose his patch and his life if he tries to step in between Alan and me. I'm not worth the fight.

"You stay in this fucking room," Alan barks out over his shoulder. "I'll be back."

He slams the door behind him and locks it, imprisoning me inside. I scramble for the door, jerking and twisting the handle to no avail. I'm trapped in here. Truly trapped.

Hours seem to tick by, but there's no sign of Alan, or anyone else for that matter. The clubhouse is eerily quiet for this time of day. I fall asleep at some point, then the roaring engines of several motorcycles snaps me awake, only to fade away after a few minutes. Did they leave?

I sit still for a bit with my ear against the door, listening. Hearing nothing, not even the music that's usually playing, I push up from the floor and stretch, trying to force the ache in my hips and back to dissipate.

Either they're outside or they're all gone... This could be my chance! I test the doorknob. It's unlocked. Could this be a test of my loyalty? Could Alan be lying in wait on the other side of the door to see what I'll do? I consider it, but decide against staying put. Listening to Alan was only going to get me one thing, and that was assaulted when he got back. I'd rather take my chances out there than wait for what's coming from him in here.

With a deep breath, I turn the knob and peer out into the hallway. No one. I silently pad down the hallway. The main room is also empty. Where in the hell did everyone go? Did they really leave me here alone?

I step over to the kitchen area for a better vantage point to the cells. Still, no one. I notice that day has come and gone when I see darkness outside the big window by the kitchen. How long was I in that room? The digital clock near the back door reads two in the morning. Jesus. It's been over fifteen hours since I went into the cells for the first time.

The kinder prospect who normally stands guard is missing. Something big must've happened for the entire club to roll out. When that's happened before, they've locked the girls away in their rooms until they returned. So, the guys have caged the girls.

I'm really confused when I find the door to the cells ajar. Either they took off in a hurry, or the door didn't latch properly when the last person in here left. Not wanting to look a gift horse in the mouth, I slip inside, careful to close the door without locking it, just as I found it. If they come back and take a quick peek, no one will be the wiser.

I head toward the occupied cell and find Priest. Peering up at me from his cot, I see the fresh blood smeared along his face.

"You came back," he rasps, looking down at my empty hands. "Can you help me?"

"I'm sorry I didn't bring you water like I promised. It's a miracle I could come back at all."

His kind eyes stare back at me. "I appreciate whatever help you can give me." He goes on to ask, "What sort of name is Boo? I've been wondering that since you left. Nickname?"

I frown. "It's the only name I've ever known. That's what I remember my uncle calling me before all of this happened. No middle or last name—just Boo."

He tries to shift from his cot, but his body gives out and he falls back like a lump.

"What sort of name is Priest?" I ask, moving forward to help him.

"Nickname. My brothers thought it would be appropriate since I used to be one."

I pause. "You were a priest? How did a priest end up in a motorcycle club?"

"Long story. Better saved for when I'm not behind bars, and you're not being watched." He laughs, but it sounds wrong. "I'd thank you properly for the gift you brought me earlier, but it's a little hard to stand."

I arch my brow. Is he trying to make a joke about his situation? He's lucky to be alive, and he's making light of his strength? Did they knock a screw loose?

"I'm not sure when I can do that again."

"Because your boyfriend might walk in?" he asks. "He didn't look too happy to find you in here earlier."

"He's not my boyfriend," I huff, looking down at floor. "He's my captor."

"Captor?"

"You're not the only prisoner in this place." He glances down at my monitoring bracelet. "I'm a slave here," I confess. "My uncle sold me to them as a child when he couldn't pay his debts."

Priest stares at me, his eyes taking in the scars buried beneath the fresh bruises on my arms. "They obviously beat you. Do they rape you?"

I swallow. I've never spoken so openly about my

captivity to another living soul, but if I want his help, he needs to know my situation. "They rape all of us. Some of the girls are just more willing to adapt than others."

Priest curses inaudibly under his breath. Anger comes off of him in waves as he forces himself to stand from the cot. His legs shake beneath him, and he has to use the wall to help him move closer to the front of the cell where I'm now standing, his chest heaving from the labor of his motions.

"He hits you," he whispers as he draws closer.

I reach up, touching the tender spot where Alan had struck me earlier. "He gets off on hurting me." My voice trembles at the admission. "It's the same for all of us. If we comply, they'll reward us with less beatings and more chores."

His hand reaches for my face, but when I recoil from his touch, he drops it. "You want out, don't you? That's why you're helping me, with the extra food and stuff?"

"I want out of here more than anything," I reply, hope filling my chest. Stupid fucking *hope*. "But you're no help to me in your condition. You can barely stand. And by the smell of you, I'd say something is getting infected."

"You need to call my club president. That's the only way either one of us is getting out of here."

My heart sinks to the floor. Making a phone call is a huge risk. "Is that our only option?"

"I was alone when they grabbed me," he grits out, his

voice laced with pain. "My club doesn't know where I am, or they'd already be busting down that fucking door. You call him, they'll come."

"I don't have a phone," I admit, the budding hope I'd been feeling mutating into dread. "Getting access to one is impossible."

"Make it possible," he urges. "Without that call, neither of us are leaving."

I hesitate. Why, I don't fucking know. The answer to my prayers is literally standing in front of me with an offer of escape, and I'm hesitating. What the hell is wrong with me? I should be jumping at this chance.

My mind races through the possibilities. I could get a phone and get caught. Alan would likely kill me. Or I could get a phone and not get caught. Either way, Alan will eventually kill me. That's a fate I've always known as an inevitability.

"I'll try."

Priest stares at me for a long moment, and then he nods. "Can you remember a number?"

"Yes."

He rattles off a number. I repeat it back to him, and he says it again. We do this back and forth, reciting the number several times before he seems satisfied.

"You call that number, tell Judge where I am, and he'll come. He'll get us both out of here."

The faint rumble of motorcycles outside reverberates off the stone walls. They're back.

"I have to go," I squeak, fear flooding every cell in my body. "If they find me in here, they'll kill us both."

I turn to run, but Priest reaches out and gently grabs my wrist, his eyes boring into mine. "Call Judge."

"I'll try." I choke out the words before bolting from the cells. I run at full speed, barely making it into the hallway when the hinges on the back-door creak open.

Fuck. Fuck. Fuck.

I pick up my speed, careful to make my footsteps as light as possible. The heavy stomps of several pairs of riding boots echo from inside the main room.

Quietly, I close the door behind me, my chest heaving from the exertion while I repeat the phone number over and over in my head.

Chapter 7

PRIEST

THE DOOR to my cell flings open with force, the metal banging against the wall as I'm stumbling toward the cot. Several members of the Screwballs storm inside, Big Dick leading the charge.

"Where the fuck are they, motherfucker?"

My eyes dart from face to face, burning each one into my memory. These are faces of the men who buy children as slaves, who have beaten and raped innocent women. These are also faces of the men I intend to destroy one by one.

Big Dick's hand flies out and clutches the front of my shirt, yanking me to him. I can't help but grin as he looks up at me, his face filled with rage and authority, regardless of the fact that I still tower over the stupid fuck.

"Where's my fucking kid?" he roars.

His question sets off hope in my heart. If he still hasn't found Harrison, that means TK was successful in getting Cora and her son to Texas. They're with the club, and they're safe.

"Raping a young girl and getting her pregnant doesn't make you the father to her kid," I say, standing taller, my shirt stretching in his fist as I get to my full height. "It makes you a fucking rapist and a piece of shit."

His eyes are black. Evil. The type of eyes some could say look possessed. But the only thing Big Dick is possessed with is his own vile spirit. The spirit of a man who already has a one-way ticket to hell, and I intend to send him there. Soon.

"Get his arms," he orders, his obsidian eyes never wavering from mine.

Two men step forward and grasp my arms, attempting to stretch them out and hold me in place, but I won't go down easily. I shake the pair off, my head swimming from the quick movement, my body betraying me as pain takes over from my previous beating. I struggle against their grip, my fists coming out to fight back, but my strength is already so depleted, the effort is futile. In the end, I lose, and it takes four of them to hold me in place.

Once I'm immobile, Big Dick steps forward. "My

patience with you is gone, Preacher. I want my kid. Where are they?"

I smirk, even though it hurts to do so with my split lips. "Safe."

His fist slams into the center of my gut while he roars in frustration. My body folds in on itself as I struggle to breathe. The men holding me up are having a hell of a time keeping me upright with Big Dick landing blow after blow into my torso, screaming and throwing a tantrum more fitting to a three-year-old than the president of any MC.

"Tell me where he took them!" he screams, spittle flying from his lips.

His eyes are wide, filled with nothing more than rage. I should be terrified. I could die before Boo even gets to make that call. He could kill me right now, stopping me from helping her and the other women here. But I'm not afraid.

Yes, I'm struggling, my lungs are burning, and the pain coursing through my body would level a weaker man. But my mind is suddenly as clear as a bell as I force myself to stand tall once more, dragging the four men at my arms with me as I do.

"That boy and his mother don't belong to you." I have to force the words out around my heaving breaths, but he hears me loud and clear. "Nobody belongs to you."

Big Dick's nostrils flare, the veins in his temples throbbing as he calculates his next move. His restraint surprises me. I would've expected him to lash out, but he knows he has to play it smart. His club is watching his every move, meaning his reputation as a club president is on the line.

I hold his glare as he reaches for his belt. Is this it? Is he going to shoot me?

But it's not a gun he removes from the holster there— it's a blade. A curved, vicious looking buck knife.

Walking behind me, he orders his men, "Hold his arms out straight."

I fight against them, and two more come, helping the others to pull my arms out at my sides.

"Your club took my kid." His voice is behind me, right at my ear, as the tip of his blade bites into the back of my neck. "Your club is finished."

The knife moves, but instead of driving it into my neck, he moves it down my leather cut, tugging with every inch. The tip of the blade nicks my skin as it moves, but it's not until he flashes the blade across my shoulder and moves to the other that I realize what he's done.

He's sliced my leather cut down the middle, then along each shoulder seam. The leather falls away in two pieces, landing on the ground with a sick thunk on each side.

Rage washes over me, but a seventh man steps behind me, this one wrapping an arm around my throat as I struggle to get at Big Dick.

"Your club is going to die, every last one of you," he says, bending to pick up both pieces of leather. The threads of my Black Hoods MC patch are tattered and torn where he's sliced through the center.

He drops the pieces back onto the floor in front of me and reaches for his zipper. "I'll kill you all, one by one, and piss on your dead bodies."

Watching in horror, he pulls out his dick and pisses on my ruined leather cut. The heavy patter of his urine is the only sound in the room. This act is the ultimate disrespect in our world, and even his own men seem shocked.

"Your turn," he tells the man behind him. Alan. The one Boo is most afraid of.

I struggle to break free as he too steps forward and pisses on the soggy remnants of my cut. I glare at him, hatred boiling in my gut.

One by one, the Screwballs take turns holding me as they step forward to repeat the deed on the disfigured Black Hoods patch, until the only one left is a scrawny guy with greasy hair and a missing front tooth.

Alan smirks. "You're up, Nutsy."

Nutsy reaches for his zipper, but instead of pulling out his dick, he drops his pants to his knees and squats over the piss pile.

"Fucking gross," somebody mutters through a laugh.

I see red as the greasy fuck winks up at me and proceeds to shit directly onto my cut. A couple of the guys gag and step out of the cell while the others chuckle, their amused gazes focused on me.

As Nutsy yanks his pants back up, Big Dick steps forward, his evil grin filled with triumph. "I'm going to end the Black Hoods. And when I'm done, Cora and Harrison will be with me, whether that bitch wants it or not."

I have no words. I look past him to the disgusting pile of human waste on the floor, the pain in my body long forgotten.

"Chain him back up," he barks, nodding to the guys behind me.

I don't bother struggling as they chain my wrists and ankles to the bonds I was in before. I can't believe any of this is actually fucking happening.

"I'll be back," Big Dick warns, already moving toward the door. "If you don't want to end up like your cut, you'll tell me where your clubhouse is and how I can get my kid."

"Fuck you," I sneer, my rage thrumming through my body like electricity.

Big Dick cackles, waiting for the room to clear so we're the only ones left.

"Sweet dreams, Preacher."

And with that, he closes the door, leaving me chained and immobile, with the smell of shit clogging my nostrils, and what was left of any hope I was hanging on to.

Chapter 8

BOO

"DID YOU TRY TO CONTACT JUDGE?" Priest asks as soon as I approach the cell with his morning gruel. It's early, and most of the club is still sleeping off last night's bender. He stands and moves closer, his voice low and urgent. "Did you?"

"I'm sorry," I whisper, peering over my shoulder to make sure I wasn't followed. "I haven't been able to find a phone."

Priest's disappointment is written all over his face. The swelling is a bit less today. His dark facial hair is more defined along his jawline, no longer hidden away by blood and bruises.

"Keep trying," he pleads.

I place the tray on the floor and slide it inside. "What do they want with you anyway?"

"They want a kid," he replies, sounding defeated.

"Big Dick's kid," I say. I'd heard them talking about the boy. "Why did your club take his kid?" Was his club like the Screwballs, trafficking kids instead of stolen women?

"We didn't." He drops back down onto the cot. "One of my brothers met the kid's mom back in Sturgis, and they're together. Big Dick assaulted her years ago, and the kid was the result. He wasn't supposed to know about him."

"Oh," I mutter, my stomach churning less than it was before. They're protecting the boy. That's a good sign. If I can get us out of here, maybe they'll be able to protect me too.

"We're not like them, Boo. Far from it. My club takes out fuckers like the Screwballs." His tone is reassuring, but when so many people let you down, it's hard to extend that olive branch of trust again.

A noise comes from the hallway. I whip my head around, sure that Alan will be standing there. We both watch in silence, but no one comes through the door.

"You can trust me, Boo," he whispers. "Help me get out of here, and I promise, we'll get you out too."

I want to believe his words with every fiber of my being, but that rescue hinges on someone being stupid enough to leave their phone both unattended and unlocked. I haven't seen anyone do that once. Not even Alan. When he takes me to his room, he locks his phone and gun in the drawer next to him with a passcode. It's impossible to crack. Believe me, I've tried many times.

"I want to help, but like I told you, finding a phone isn't going to be easy."

Another bang outside the locked door to the hallway. Someone's coming, signaling that my time is up. Getting caught in here, talking to Priest, isn't going to help either of us.

"I have to go," I mutter, skirting away and rushing down the hall toward the sound. I peer back at Priest over my shoulder before closing the door. A hopeful, almost pleading look is on his face as he watches me.

I'm placing the key back on its hook when a voice observes, "Been in there a while," causing me to nearly jump out of my skin.

The prospect who's usually so nice to me is there, sitting on a stool propped up against the wall outside the entrance to the cells. I stay silent, unsure of what to say, so I opt for saying nothing at all and head back to the main room. Alan's eyes lock onto mine as soon as I step inside. He stalks toward me, an unreadable expression on his face.

"Was he awake?"

"No," I lie. "I just dropped off his food and left. He was still asleep, I think. Didn't move."

"Good," he grunts. "He won't be taking up your time here much longer."

My heart plummets, but I stop my reaction to his words before anything shows on my face. "Is someone else going to be taking over?"

"No," he says with a dark chuckle. "Get going on your chores." His fingers move up, playing with the solitary braid hanging over my right shoulder, like an enamored boyfriend would do. "I have plans for us tonight. I've missed my little mouse."

I shiver at the thought. I've had a reprieve the last few days with the club's business taking his attention. I'd been able to sleep in my own bed—well, pallet—and I haven't been woken up by his disgusting evening pursuits with my body. Part of me has held out that he'd lost interest in me, and that they'd brought in another girl he liked better. But naivety was never one of my strong suits. His disinterest isn't fleeting.

With a painful slap to my ass, Alan sends me on my way.

I tackle cleaning up the kitchen from breakfast, stealing a few scraps off some of the plates as I wash them in the large kitchen sink, all while playing Alan's words about Priest over and over in my mind. *He won't be taking up your time here much longer.* What did he mean?

Most of the girls are making themselves scarce this morning. Judging from the sounds I'd heard coming from the club's rooms last night, they'd been busy.

Tammy is the only one looking bright-eyed and bushy-tailed this morning, slinking out of Big Dick's room with a sly smile on her face. Instead of doing her part of the chores, she's been attached to Big Dick's side, nestled up on one of the large sofas in the center of the room.

Every time I leave the kitchen to gather more plates from the tables, she shoots me a surly grin. She's happy to be used. How she can be okay with her situation makes zero sense to me. I know there's something called Stockholm syndrome, which is something someone can get when they're in an unsafe situation. Self-preservation, they call it. But she's been here only a few more months than I have. I hadn't broken, but maybe she had.

Spying one last pile of dishes on the far away table, I move to grab them, but watch from the corner of my eye as Alan joins Big Dick on the couch. Tammy's face falls when they dismiss her, and she stomps off toward our rooms. Trying to focus on the dishes, and seeing that I'm still doing my chores, I move a little closer to them.

"Anything new today?" Big Dick asks Alan.

"Not a fucking thing. Motherfucker hasn't said shit since last night."

"Bastard," Big Dick mutters. "If he's not going to be useful to us alive, he will be when he's dead."

Alan grins. "What do you think they'll do when we send his body back to them, wrapped up in a pretty bow?"

Big Dick's laughter is loud and quick, startling me as I wipe down a nearby table. "They'll finally know who they're messing with. I'm gonna get my boy back one way or another, and dismantle that fucking club one member at a time, starting with Cora. I'll make that big bastard she's with watch as I take back what's mine."

Alan nods. "Can't fucking wait. Austin is primo territory. We take the mother chapter, the others will have to fall in line."

"Damn right," someone adds to the conversation. "Fuck the Black Hoods."

The rest of the men echo the same phrase together. Alan notices me, his eyes narrowing as I work, pretending like I've heard nothing. But I did hear. I heard it all.

Priest's life is going to end if I don't do something fast. If they kill Priest, his blood will be on my hands too, because I could have stopped it.

I'll stop it. No matter what, I will stop it.

Silently, I return to the kitchen to finish the dishes, my mind racing to come up with a plan that won't get both Priest and me killed. I come up with nothing.

Several minutes later, knowing I don't have much time to collect the laundry, I turn to find Alan standing silently behind me, his large body leaning against the counter by the door as he tracks my every move.

"Jesus, Alan," I squeal, pressing a hand to my chest as if to contain my heart from flying out of it.

Alan smirks. "I'm not Jesus. I'm much more than that."

If he's God, I don't want to live on this plane of existence anymore.

"You startled me."

"I'm sure I did. I like watching you work, Boo. Almost as much as I like watching you squirm while I fuck you."

I open my mouth to respond, but stop myself before the snark can flow past my lips. I can't be punished, not today. I need to get to a phone, and I can't do that if I'm locked up.

Alan shoves off the counter, and with three wide strides, meets me on my side of the kitchen. "Playtime, my little mouse. Gonna be a busy few days. Come with me." He reaches down, removing the wet dish towel from my hands, and drags me out of the room.

He leads me down the hall and into his room, locking the door behind me after he pulls me inside. The second the door locks, he's on me. His hands grip my waist, shoving me back against the doorframe. His lips descend onto my neck. I'm already chanting my regular mantra in my mind as his hands roam over my body.

He shifts us to the bed, throwing me onto it with a bounce while he stares down at me. I meet his glare, knowing I have to play it cool, and act like I always do. I can't back down. I've never backed down. Not once in all these years have I ever let him see what's going on in my head while he rapes me. I won't give him my emotions. I won't let him see that every time he does this, he steals a part of my soul. I must have so little soul left now.

"Fuck, I love it when you stare at me like that." This is the only time he allows me to go against him. He gets off on my disobedience in the bedroom. "Those eyes of yours are so full of fire."

He tugs at my jeans, not even bothering to unbutton them. The material bites into my hips as he works them down with my underwear, then throws them onto the floor. Without warning, he flips me onto my stomach. The sound of him unzipping his pants behind me is the only warning I have before he's inside of me.

One Mississippi. Two Mississippi. Three Mississippi. Four....

One hundred... One hundred and one.

Time blurs as I let my mind drift away from reality. I block out what's happening, because I learned a long time ago that it's the only way. My own version of self-preservation. If my mind isn't here, it's only my body that must be present. I think of good things, like puppies and beaches, and the little boy I barely remember from my childhood. Anything I can think of that makes my heart smile, floats through my mind until finally, he grunts and rolls off of me.

Without a word, Alan marches off to his adjoining bathroom, leaving me naked on the bed. I wait for the door to close before going in search of my jeans. I find them by his nightstand, and when I bend down to get them, I notice something odd. The drawer where Alan keeps his cell phone is ajar. The corner of his bedding is caught in the corner of the drawer, preventing it from latching.

My heart flutters as I peek inside. His phone is there. There's no gun, but the phone is what I *really* need right now.

Oh my God.

The blood in my veins whooshes through my ears as I slip my hand inside the drawer, my eyes glued to the bathroom door. Hands trembling, I wrap my fingers around the phone and pull it out of the drawer when I hear the shower turning on.

The screen lights up, but it's asking for a password.

Shit. Shit. Shit.

I don't have the slightest idea what it could be. I don't know his birthday, or any other number that would be special to him. I study the greasy screen, but no pattern is left on the glass. It's a fucking mess.

Think, Boo… Think! This could be my only shot.

That's when it hits me—Alan's tattoos! Mostly a mix

of naked pin-up girls and biker shit, but the one on his chest? The one all his other tattoos are centered around? Aren't there numbers inside of it? Yes! His mom's birthday. He'd mentioned it once, how it was his first tattoo.

My hands tremble as I press those numbers onto the screen. One. Zero. Two. Four. Five. Four. The lock screen disappears, and the background with little squares pops up in its place.

Holy fuck, it worked! I've never used a phone before. I've never been allowed to use any kind of technology, other than a television remote. How do you make a call on these damn things?

With the shower still hissing from the other room, I scan the screen. Finally, I see a small green square with a phone on it, and when I touch it, a telephone touch pad pops up.

My entire body quakes with nerves as I dial the number Priest had given me. It rings and rings, but on the fifth ring, a gruff voice answers, "Hello?"

"They have Priest," I whisper into the phone, my hand cupping the receiver to muffle my voice.

"Speak up," he growls. "I can barely hear you. Did you say Priest?"

My heart pounds faster as I remove my hand from the receiver, trying to calm my nerves so I can speak more clearly. "Screwballs MC. They have Priest. They're going to kill him."

"Who is this?"

"My name is B—"

The phone is ripped from my hands. Looking up, I find Alan standing over me, seething, as he presses the phone to his ear. "Who is this?" he snarls.

Judge must not answer him, because he repeats the question three more times before he throws his phone across the room.

"Who the fuck did you just call?" he roars, shaking me by the shoulders.

I don't say a word. It doesn't matter, because I'd done it. I'd called Judge, and now he knows where Priest is. Now he can save him and the others, even if it's too late for me.

Alan's face is red with rage as he rears his head back and slams it into my face. The entire world fades away with a crack. I sink into the darkness, knowing I might not wake up this time, but I'd done what I could, and it was worth it.

Chapter 9

PRIEST

MY BODY SCREAMS in pain with every move I make. I don't know how long it's been since Boo last came to my room, but if I'm judging by the meals delivered to my room, I'd say it's been three days now.

The bleach blonde woman delivering my one meal a day appears to be in her mid-twenties, but she looks rough, aging before her time. Her face is lined with slight wrinkles, and her make-up is far too thick. She looks like a painted lady. One trying to distract someone from really looking too closely.

The first couple of times she came, I was too weak to say anything. The last beating those bastards gave me had done some serious damage. Ribs are definitely broken. And if the bruise growing on my side is any indication, I have internal bleeding. My time is drawing near, and I know I won't survive another beating.

Footsteps approach from the hallway. I watch the door, praying it's Boo coming this time. It's not.

The woman steps up to the bars, pausing when she notices me watching her. As if I could get out of this bed to get at her if I wanted to.

Satisfied I'm not going to charge at her, she pushes the tray into my cell and turns to leave.

"Boo," I croak out, my voice thick and cracked.

The blonde stops in her tracks, her eyes flashing to mine. "What did you say?"

"Where's Boo?"

The woman studies me for a moment, her eyes calculated and cruel. "Not sure you're supposed to know her name, asshole, but that bitch got what was coming to her. She won't be back."

She says this with an air of satisfaction, as if she hadn't just delivered the news that nearly stopped my struggling heart. *She won't be back.* What does that mean? Did they kill her?

I know I've already fucked up by saying her name. Blondie's right, I shouldn't have known that, and Boo will pay for my error. *If she's even alive to make that payment.*

"What did they do to her?" I ask, attempting to push myself into a sitting position, and failing. Pain rips through my abdomen, and it takes every ounce of strength I have in me not to scream in agony. But I won't.

I won't give any fucker here, including this evil bitch, the satisfaction of hearing the pain they've caused me.

Blondie doesn't answer at first, her eyes assessing my reaction. Finally, she grins. "What's the matter, Preacher? Did Boo turn you on? Did she fuck you like she fucks everyone else around here?"

Her words attack my mind like acid, burning visions of Boo being raped over and over again because I'd asked her to help me.

Blondie steps forward, close enough to touch if I were able to get up. "Boo's gone now, but you're in luck. You get me." Her hands come up to her breasts, fondling them through her shirt. "I can fuck you much better than Boo ever could. You want me to fuck you, Preacher?"

I gape at her in horror. How is this real? I've come across countless men in my life who had no conscience or goodness in them, but until now, I've never met a woman so vile.

"Tammy," Big Dick snaps from down the hall. "Get the fuck out of here. Now."

Winking, Tammy drops her hands and breezes past Big Dick without a care in the world.

"You should know we found your clubhouse," Big Dick says, leaning against the bars. "Friend of mine is there now, watching their every move, and your stupid club doesn't have a clue."

Hopeless defeat crushes against my chest like a lead

weight. Big Dick found the clubhouse, Boo is mysteriously missing, and I can't even sit up, let alone rip this motherfucker's head off.

Big Dick's face splits into a grin. He knows he has me. He knows this news is tearing me apart.

"Don't worry, Preacher. Your time is nearly up. You won't even be around to see the war."

I don't respond. I can't. I can't breathe. I can't move. I can't help my fucking club. The only thing I can do is lie here in agony and pray that Boo is okay, and that she found a way to contact Judge.

Even his life may depend on that.

Chapter 10

BOO

THE DARKNESS SLIPS AWAY, but I can't open my eyes. A thick crust sticks to my eyelashes. I try to wipe it away, but it takes several attempts before I can peel my eyelids apart. I blink once. Twice. Light flickers back into my vision.

Raising my hands, I stare at the dried, crumbly blood covering them. That's what was crusting my eyes closed. Trailing my fingertips along my face, I find more trails of dried blood. God, Alan had gotten me good this time. He'd been out for blood. This was not the sick torture he liked to call foreplay.

My body aches as I try to shift. My muscles scream from lack of movement and the need for more rest, all at the same time. How many hours or days had passed, I didn't know. But the waves of agony and the damp feeling of piss between my legs tells me it's been days.

It's not until I try to stand that I notice the thick chain around my ankle and the collar around my neck. New accessories I don't remember adding to my outfit. Alan's handiwork, no doubt. He'd threatened me once with a punishment of this sort, by chaining me to his bed and never letting me leave. I guess it wasn't a threat after all.

I tug at my bonds. The chains are heavy, making it impossible to move in my weakened state. My heart plummets as despair fills my soul. I'm well and thoroughly trapped.

"You're awake," Alan's voice calls from the doorway. "About fucking time." Sauntering into the room, his sinister grin grows the closer he gets, like a cat stalking its prey.

"Sorry to keep you waiting," I snap, my hope at escape so diminished, I no longer care to keep up the facade of being a willing participant in this fucked-up situation. Alan had caught me red handed with that phone, and I knew the consequences if I got caught— death, or being sold. Two options that honestly don't seem so bad, given the situation I'm in right now.

"You always did have a mouth on you." Pausing in front of me, he snags my chin between his fingers. "You could burn a man to death with that glare of yours."

Alan would be ash in the wind if that were possible. They would all be.

"Tell me, does your head hurt?"

I glare at him.

"Answer me," he growls, spittle spraying across my face like a rogue shower nozzle. He digs his fingers deeper into my flesh.

"Yes," I hiss, just wanting the added pain to go away.

"Good," he smiles before releasing me. "Be a good girl, and tell me who you were trying to call."

"Nobody."

His fist slams into my cheek. The impact forces me to stumble back, the chain around my throat and foot clanking with the motion. I fall to the ground, but don't stay there long, as Alan hauls me to my feet and tosses me onto the bed.

My back hits the mattress with a bounce, and I watch Alan through narrow, tear-filled eyes, Alan straddling the lower half of my body that's hanging off the bed, keeping me in place like he's done so many times. I doubt his cock will come into play this time, though. He's here for blood—my blood.

"Tell me the truth, you lying bitch." He punches me again, this time in the stomach. I try to curl away from the impact to protect myself, but Alan stops me by grabbing the chain connected to my collar and jerking it. "Who. Were. You. Calling?"

"Wouldn't you like to know?" I choke out, the collar pressing against my windpipe. I know my response will piss him off, but if these are to be my last minutes on earth, I'd rather spend them fighting back than submitting like I've done since I was sold to this godforsaken club. No more. I'm done pretending. I'm done letting shit happen to me because that's the way it's supposed to be. It's not the way it's supposed to be. And even if I only have a few precious breaths left, I'll take them while fighting this cocksucker.

"Your little mouse disobeyed you. How does that feel, Alan? The betrayal of trust. I bet you're wondering how many times it's happened. Would you like to know that answer? Dozens. With all of your fucking brothers. That's who I was calling. I was begging one of your brothers to come and save me from having to deal with your pencil dick."

It's a lie. They hadn't touched me, but he didn't know that. It's clearly been days since the call, and Alan's inquisition leads me to the fact that he doesn't know I called Priest's club. I have no idea how, but it's clear he doesn't. And if he doesn't know, they could be on their way to get Priest, to get me—*if* I survive this.

And if I don't survive? At least Priest has a chance to escape, and his club could put an end to the Screwballs MC once and for all. That in itself would be worth the price I paid.

"Fucking bitch!" Alan's hands clench around my

throat, squeezing and blocking air from entering or exiting my lungs. I thrash, my hands and knees flailing, trying to make a connection with his balls. Alan just presses his body into mine, using his weight to squeeze my legs together. "Tell me!"

"No," I wheeze, the word barely audible.

He squeezes and squeezes, his eyes bulging from his head as he stares down at me with rage and hatred. The world grows dimmer, but just as the light completely fades away, the pressure disappears.

I gasp, choking on gasps of air as I claw my way up the bed, away from him.

"I told you not to fucking kill her, Alan," Big Dick roars from somewhere in the room. I look over and see him leaning against the doorframe, while two club members hold Alan back by his arms.

"If you knew what she did, you wouldn't be saying that," Alan spits back before stopping himself.

Big Dick arches his brow as he looks at me. "What did she do exactly?"

Alan peers over at me before turning his attention back to his president. After a few moments of silence, he grunts, "Fucking bitch spit in my face and kicked me in the balls."

What? Why is Alan lying to his president? Did he really not tell him that I broke the rules?

He didn't tell Big Dick. He caught me red-handed, and he didn't immediately run off to report me like a narc? But why? He's Big Dick's little lap dog, ready and willing to do whatever he tasks him to do.

"And?" Big Dick inquires, tilting his head to the side. "You get off on that shit."

"She got me good this time," Alan mutters. "With everything going on, I lost my shit."

Big Dick stares him down before finally nodding. "Remember the rules with this one," he says, pointing to where I lay frozen on the bed. "If you break it, I break my foot off in your ass. You can't kill her. Am I crystal fucking clear on that?"

"Yes, Prez," Alan grumbles.

"Good. Boys, let him go." They quickly release him, leaving him rubbing at his arms, as if brushing their germs off his skin. Stabbing a finger in Alan's face, Big Dick advises, "I won't warn you again. Keep her alive."

"I will," he replies, sounding more like the trained animal he is.

"Good. Now get your ass to the meeting room. We've got some guests arriving later today, and we need to discuss strategy." Big Dick looks over at me once more and frowns. "And get her fucking cleaned up while you're at it. It smells like a fucking urinal in here."

Without a second glance, Big Dick stalks out of the

room with the other guys on his heels. Alan stays behind.

"I'll send in one of the girls to get you cleaned up," he snarls through clenched teeth. And with that, he leaves the room.

Chapter 11

PRIEST

"HEY THERE, HANDSOME," Tammy purrs, stepping up to the bars. She's wearing a barely-there black skirt, and a shirt that looks more like a bra than a functional piece of actual clothing. Her hips sway as she moves, a coy smile playing on her lips as she looks me up and down. "You look like you could use some comfort."

The tone in her voice sours my stomach. She's here for a purpose, and I would bet my life that it has nothing to do with the Screwballs.

"How much longer are you fuckers gonna drag this out?" I ask, pushing myself up to a sitting position on the cot.

Several days have passed now, and I'm beginning to regain a bit of my strength, though the pain is getting worse. I haven't seen Boo again, and I'm pretty sure she never got the chance to make that phone call. Is she even still alive? Did she get caught trying to help me?

Either way, the guilt of her disappearance weighs heavily on my heart and mind. That girl has been through so much, and she'd told me how dangerous it would be to sneak a phone call. I hadn't listened. I'd been so intent on my own survival, I'd failed at helping ensure hers.

Tammy pokes her lower lip out in an exaggerated pout. "Oh, that's not very nice. I just came to give you some company."

Even from the other side of the locked bars, she looms over where I sit on the cot, and I don't like the upper hand it gives her. Biting back the pain, I force myself to stand and step up to the bars. At my full height, I tower over her. "I'd rather be alone."

Shaking her head, she reaches for a ribbon on the material between her breasts. "I bet you wouldn't say that if I was Boo."

I glare down at her as she tugs at the ribbon. It loosens and falls away, her bare breasts popping free. "You're not Boo."

Anger flashes in her dull, gray eyes. "I'm better than Boo," she coos, stepping closer, her nipples brushing against the metal bars.

I have never laid a finger on a woman, but I've also

never had such a hateful woman in my space before. "Not interested."

Tammy ignores my words; she doesn't care. Instead, she shrugs her shirt off completely and slides her skirt down over her hips. She's naked now, and the anger in her gaze is more than just anger... it's predatory.

"You think Boo would make you feel as good as I can?"

Reaching her arms through the rungs of the cell, her hands go for my belt. As soon as her fingers make contact with the buckle, I grip her wrists in my hands and push her back a step. "Where is she?" I ask. I know I shouldn't even say her name. She'll get into trouble if they know I'm asking for her. But I know Tammy is here on her own, and if the men caught her, she'd be in for a world of hurt. She's not going to tell them, unless she wants them to know she had snuck in.

Tammy's lips curl in disgust. "Fuck that pink-haired bitch. Why do you fucking men make such a fuss over her? She's a whiny little slut who thinks she's better than the rest of us."

Yanking her wrists from my grasp, she reaches in with her right hand and cups me between my legs. "I can make you feel better than she ever could," she says, her palm massaging along my soft length. "I can make you forget about this place, just for a little while."

"Where. Is. Boo?" I ask through clenched teeth.

She continues to massage my cock, but she's not getting anywhere. I'd rather fuck a rusty stump grinder than put my dick anywhere near her.

"If I tell you, what will you do for me?" Reaching in with her other hand once more, she unbuckles my belt as she speaks, her eyes cast up to look at me from beneath her fake lashes.

My mind races. Maybe she has the key. Maybe if I do this, she'll unlock the door and I could make a run for it. Lock Tammy in this room and sneak out before anyone even notices I'm gone. But could I? I can barely stand, let alone run. And what about Boo? I can't just leave her here. I can't escape without her.

Or I could play along, get some information out of her. Maybe even talk her into helping me get out of here.

Battling back the bile brewing in my gut, I force a grin, my split lips stretching wide as I pull my belt through the loops of my jeans and open my fly. Tammy grins, her teeth sinking into her lower lip as she pulls my cock free.

"You gonna fuck me, Preacher?"

"Where's Boo?" I ask again, my voice softer this time.

Tammy strokes my length, her thumb skimming over the top, trying to get me hard. It's not working. "Do you know that none of the guys here can make me come?" she says instead, not answering my question. "I've only ever came when I touch myself. Can you make me come, Preacher?"

This evil bitch is sick, but I need to know about Boo. I need to know if she's okay, and if she made that call to Judge.

Finally, shoving my disgust down into the deepest depths of my stomach, I reach through the bars and roll her nipple between my fingers, giving it a light pinch. "Tell me where she is," I whisper.

Tammy's head rolls back and she moans. "Make me come, and I'll tell you."

I may have been a priest back in the day, but I'm no virgin. I'm also not one of those guys who can just fuck any old bitch with a pussy. Sex, to me, is more than just an itch to scratch. It's a meeting of two souls. A connection. Tammy is the last woman on earth I'd ever want to be connected to.

But she could be my only hope.

I drop my hand, trailing my fingertips along her belly, then down through her thick curls and into the wet center between her thighs. I shove my actions from my mind and slide my finger through her folds, pausing to rub her swollen nub.

Tammy's body trembles, and she squeezes my cock a bit tighter as she continues to stroke me. I'm still not growing any harder. Possibly because I may have to cut this entire hand off after touching her nasty cunt.

"Keep going," she insists, her hands releasing me and coming up to rest on my shoulders.

I continue to rub her, the pad of my thumb rolling around her clit as I force my brain to disconnect from this vile act.

Don't think about it, dude. Just get her off and find out where Boo is.

Tammy's fingers dig into my shoulders as she rocks her hips, grinding her clit into my hand. "Put your finger inside me."

I do as she tells me, wanting nothing more than to get this over with. Tammy gasps, her hips rocking faster, her moans growing louder with each thrust against my hand.

"What the fuck?"

Tammy jumps back and whips around as Big Dick enters my field of view, his brow furrowed as he takes in the scene.

"Big Dick," Tammy gasps, her hands coming up to cover her tiny tits. "I was just…" She stops talking. How is she going to explain this?

"Put your fucking clothes on," Big Dicks snarls, bending down to grab her skirt from the floor and tossing it at her.

"I was just trying to get some information from him," she says, her words hurried as she rushes to get dressed. "I was trying to help."

"We don't need more information from him, you dumb bitch. We know what we need to know." He grabs her arm and yanks her toward him. "Who the fuck gave you permission to be in here?"

Tammy's fear hangs in the air like a storm cloud, growing heavier by the second. "Nobody. I…"

"Get the fuck out of here," he snaps, shoving her half-dressed ass toward the door. "I'll deal with you later."

"Big Dick, I—"

"Now!" he roars.

Tammy chokes back a sob, her eyes flashing to me before settling back on him. "I just—"

Big Dick's hand comes back, raised to strike her.

"Boo!" she screams, her body curling away, her arm coming up to protect herself. "He was asking about Boo! I just wanted to figure out why."

Big Dick pauses, his hand still in the air as he turns to face me. "Boo? Why were you asking about Boo?"

I glare at him, but don't say a word.

"He wants to know where she is," Tammy divulges, her voice calmer now. Mocking.

Big Dick stares at me, his gaze cold and cruel. "Sounds like Boo's been a naughty girl too, and not in a good way." He drops his hand and looks at me, the growing grin on his face making my knees turn to rubber. "Your time is nearly up, Preacher, but it sounds like you're about to get some company in that cold grave of yours."

Chapter 12

BOO

HOURS SLIP INTO DAYS. Well, at least, I think they do. My concept of time is gradually slipping away while I'm caged inside Alan's room. No one comes in here but him. The only exception to that is when Tammy had come in to help clean me up, per Big Dick's request. Why it had to be her, I'll never know. My luck, I guess. Her spiteful remarks over my body and the scars on it were enough to make me consider risking it all and gouging the bitch's eyes out. I'd have done it too if it weren't for Alan coming back into the room.

My next shower came under his watchful eye. There isn't enough soap in the world to wash away the disgust I felt as he palmed himself while observing me under the spray. I did my best to block it out like normal, but day after day of listening to that sick swishing sound the second I walk into the shower is the stuff of nightmares. That invasion of privacy is tame compared to the rest of my nights with him, though.

Besides the meal he brings me in the morning, just as I did for Priest, I see no one else. He lingers just long enough to ensure I've eaten, then disappears again until the next meal, or until he comes back for the night, taking my body like he owns it before collapsing onto the bed beside me.

He doesn't tell me why he lied to Big Dick about what I did. What purpose did it serve him? And why was my life more important than the other women imprisoned here? Why did my life mean so much to Big Dick? The entire thing confuses me more and more each time I try to make sense of it all, the whys coming in a constant string of implausible scenarios.

After breakfast this morning, Alan had done his disappearing act as usual, so color me surprised when I hear the door being unlocked from the outside. I peer up from my bed, only to see Tammy walking through the door.

Fucking Tammy.

"What do you want?"

"Someone's been asking about you," Tammy chirps, sauntering into the room. My heart skips a beat. Priest. Was Priest asking about me? Is he still alive?

"Who let you get up off your knees?" I ask, not

playing into her nasty little game. "They finally get tired of you?"

"Still a bitch, I see," she remarks, closing the door behind her. "I'd have thought being chained up like an animal would change your attitude, but guess not." She shrugs, still smiling like a cat that ate the canary.

"It takes more than chains to break me, Tammy."

She grins. "I doubt that."

"How many STDs do you have now?" I don't know why I'm baiting her. Maybe just because I hate her, and because I know that when she's pissed, she'll be more likely to tell me things without meaning to.

"You're just jealous," she says, her eyes narrowed, though her smile never falls. "They want me, and they don't want a mousey little pink-haired bitch like you." Jealousy? Is she for real right now? Jealous is not the word I would use for the feelings I have about her or any of them. Disgust, disdain, repugnance, aversion? Take your Webster's Dictionary pick. Jealousy will not be one of the options. "Aren't you the least bit curious as to who's been asking about you?" she goes on.

"No."

"Oh, come on, Boo." She plops down onto the bed beside me. The mattress bounces us both from the collision with her ass. She falls back next to me, peering up from her spot. "I know you want to know."

"I don't."

"You're no fun, you know that? I came here out of love and concern for your well-being, just to let you know that you're missed," she teases. "He's handsome, by the way."

Another flutter of my heart. "Who the fuck are you talking about?"

Tammy slips onto her stomach, her chin resting on the tops of her clenched hands, like a teenager gossiping with her best girlfriend about boys. "Our sexy friend in the cells."

Priest is alive. Oh, thank God.

I try to hide my relief, but Tammy must take notice, because her smile widens.

"You've been holding out on me, Boo. All this time, I thought you having to feed him was punishment for something. But you liked it, didn't you?" She bats her cheap false eyelashes at me. "Don't worry, girl, I get it. I see the appeal. He's good with his fingers too."

My gut sinks. She's lying. She must be.

"They let you feed him?" I say, keeping my voice from trembling at this new information. "I didn't think chores were your thing. Your talents lie elsewhere."

She narrows her eyes as I take in her outfit. Her tiny skirt is far too small, and barely covers her wide ass. "Why do you always dress like a horny teenager?"

"Fuck off," she hisses. "You wish you had these guys eating out of the palm of your hand like I do. I'm going to be Big Dick's woman soon, just watch. And once I'm his ol' lady, the first thing I'm going to do is get rid of you."

I bark out a laugh. "Oh, God. You're serious, aren't you? You really think he's going to put a patch on your worn-out ass? You're delusional."

Snarling, she pushes up from her position on her stomach and pounces on me like a tiger. Her weight hits me like a ton of bricks, pushing me back onto the bed. The chains from my collar tangle with her hair as I shove her back. With a hard yank, I rip them free, tearing some of her tresses from her scalp.

"You bitch! You did that on purpose!" She tries to scratch at my face with her nails, but I pull my arms up to protect my face the best I can, her voice piercing as she screams insult after insult at me. Then suddenly, a large arm wraps around her waist, pulling her away from me.

"The fuck you doin'?" Alan growls, tugging her off the bed and away from me. The fight leaves her in an instant. "Explain yourself."

Tammy looks over at me, then back to Alan, a sinister smile forming on her lips. I don't like that smile. Not one fucking bit.

"Boo's made herself a new friend, Alan. Did she tell you that?"

Alan's brow furrows. "What the fuck are you talking about?"

Tammy's smile grows wider. "The preacher's been asking about her. Seems they have a real connection."

Alan's face goes blank, and every drop of blood in my body drains to my feet. "Out," he orders her. "Get the fuck out!"

Tammy wastes no time, her heels digging into the hardwood as she pulls herself upright and hurries toward the door. "Big Dick knows," she warns. "He sent me in here. He's not happy."

And with that parting blow, she slams the door behind her. Alan stays where he's at, glaring at me.

"Is it true?" he asks, his voice low and emotionless. "Have you been talking to him?"

"No," I lie. "How could I do that from here?"

"After everything I've done for you, you're gonna sit there on my bed, breathing my fucking air, and lie to me? After what I did to save your ass?"

"I'm not lying to you," I insist, praying I sound convincing. "But why did you lie for me? Why didn't you tell Big Dick about the phone?"

Alan crosses the room in three long strides, his hands coming to the collar at my neck. He grips the chain attached to it and yanks me forward until our noses are nearly touching.

"Because I *own* you," he snarls.

"Why?" I push. "Why do you have to keep me alive? Why am I so special?"

"Special," he scoffs. "I'll show you how fucking special you are."

With rough, hurried motions, he pulls a key from his pocket and unlocks the chain at my throat, then the one at my ankle.

"Get up."

Fear holds me in place, and when I don't comply, he grabs me by the hair and yanks me off the bed. With another tug, I'm on my feet. Pain rips through my scalp, causing tears to stream down my cheeks, but I don't make a sound.

He pulls me behind him, dragging me down the hall. We hit the main room, but Alan doesn't stop. He keeps going, hauling me down the hallway until we're at the cell doors. The prospect on duty scrambles from his spot when he sees us.

"Open the fucking door!" he yells.

The prospect moves quickly, and has the door open in an instant. Alan reaches forward, grabs the bars, and yanks me through. The prospect's face falls as we pass him, his eyes filled with pity as he meets my gaze. Pity, yet no action. *Fucking coward.*

His hand still clenched around my braids, Alan pulls me along until we're just outside of Priest's cell, and then he throws me to the ground in front of it. I don't dare look up at Priest, but I feel his warm presence there. I hear his feet hit the floor from his cot, staggering to a stop in front of us.

"The fuck are you doing, man? Is she okay?"

"I heard you've been talking to my girl," Alan seethes. Gripping my hair once more, he yanks my head back, forcing me to peer up at Priest. Terror flashes in his eyes, and his jaw goes rigid when he sees my face.

"I'm not your girl," I hiss.

With an enraged growl, Alan shoves me into the bars and drags me to my feet. My face presses into the cut hard metal, my eyes locked on Priest's.

Priest lunges forward, so close now, I could touch him. "Let her go, motherfucker. She's not a part of this. You want me, not her." Panic cracks in his voice. "Boo has nothing to do with this."

Alan stiffens at my name. *Shit. Now he knows I lied.*

Priest knows my name, and he just admitted it. I'm dead. Fucking dead.

Alan's fingers dig into my scalp as he shoves my face forward, the pressure of the bars biting into my face. "This bitch is my fucking property. I'll do what I want with her. If I want to take her right now with you as an audience, I will. If I want to take her life, right here, right now, I fucking will. She's mine."

"Just let her go," Priest pleads, the fight gone from his voice.

I stare up at him, my gaze strong, trying to tell him without words that I'm okay. This isn't the first time, as

Alan forces himself on me whenever the hell he likes. He can't let Alan break him. He can't let him win.

"No," Alan growls. "I want you to watch, Preacher. You watch how she takes my cock, how she squeals when I fuck her. How she submits. You'd like that, wouldn't you, my little mouse?"

My eyes don't leave Priest's. He needs to let this happen, but the stubborn man shakes his head and steps forward, lacing his fingers through the bar to caress my index finger with his. His calming touch jerks me back to reality. If he tries to stop Alan, he'll punch his ticket to the underworld. They'll exploit me to get him to talk. I'm not worth that. I'm not worth a kid's life.

Alan releases his grip on my hair, but traps me against the bars with his body, awkwardly ripping at my clothes. The cold metal bites into my flesh as he rips and tugs, finally succeeding in getting me naked.

With no reaction, I look at Priest while Alan's hands trail down my neck, then farther south. He cups my breasts, squeezing them painfully in his grip. My breath hitches from the pain, but I don't cry out.

Priest doesn't have the same restraint, though. He roars, banging and yanking on the bars as if he can rip them from their frame. Blood streams from his knuckles as he falls apart in his cell.

I ignore what's happening to my body right now and keep my gaze trained on Priest. "Please," I say, though I don't make a sound, forming the single word with my lips.

Alan's hands reach the apex of my thighs and pushes between them, despite how hard I'm clenching them together.

"Open them, Boo," he growls into my ear. When I don't comply, he forces his knee between my legs and fumbles for his belt.

"You want information? I'll fucking give it to you," Priest shouts, no longer trying to decimate the bars, and instead, wrapping his hands around them, desperation clear in his voice.

Chuckling, Alan pauses. "Just like that, huh? You'll give up your club for a piece of pussy? Fucking pathetic."

"I'll give you what you want, but only if you let her go," he argues back. "You don't need her."

"That's where you're wrong. My little mouse is special. Let me show you just how special she is." Alan's belt smacks my bare ass as he rips it from his waist. In a flash, that belt is around my throat where the collar had been just moments ago. He tightens it, restricting my air as he grinds his cock against my ass.

"Stop!" Priest cries. "Don't fucking touch her!"

"Fuck you, Preacher. I own this bitch." Helpless to do anything, I feel his body moving behind me as he pulls down his jeans, and then, without warning, he shoves himself inside of me as far as he can go. I cry out in pain, trying to fight back. This time is different than any other time Alan has raped me. This time, he's more detached. He's going to kill me, right here and now, all to make a point to Priest.

Alan thrusts into me over and over again, yanking on the belt around my neck, forcing my head to snap back.

"Look at me, Boo," Priest whispers, his face just inches from mine through the bars. "Focus on me." I meet his sad gaze, wishing I could crawl into the kindness there and wrap myself in his warmth. "I'm sorry... I'm so fucking sorry." He repeats the sentiment again and again as Alan claims my body in front of him. All I can do is just hold his stare. My Mississippi's aren't needed when I have his face in front of me.

"She's. Fucking. Mine," Alan grunts out with each thrust, his hips slapping against me. "Mine."

"Not for long, she isn't," Priest bites back. His words are a promise to all three of us. I wish he could keep that promise, but he won't be alive long enough to do anything to help me or himself.

Alan either doesn't hear him, or is just flat-out ignoring him. He keeps going, fucking my body until my knees give out.

A tear glides down my cheek as my eyes fall closed. My body had given up long ago, but my spirit... it's slipping away.

I want to keep fighting. I want to make this stop, but I'm powerless. Humiliated. Worthless. All this time, and I'm nothing but a gash to fuck. A hole to fill.

I was delusional to think I could change my fate. That I could save this man so desperately trying to keep my focus on him instead of what's happening to me. But there's nothing left to hope for. I'm just… empty.

Chapter 13

PRIEST

MY GUT TWISTS with rage and grief as I watch Boo slide to the floor when Alan releases her, feeling so much disgust as he tucks his dick back into his pants and zips them up. He reaches for the belt around her neck and pulls it free. Boo doesn't move or make a sound.

Her eyes are open and glazed, staring up at the ceiling, but not really seeing anything at all.

Alan threads his belt through the loops of his jeans, watching me with a grin on his ugly ass face.

"I'm going to kill you," I tell him. My words are not filled with rage or hatred; they're simply a vow. I will kill him. Even if I'm going to die here in this cell, I will find a way to end this fucker's life. At least that will spare Boo from any more of his sexual deviancy.

Alan pauses as he buckles his belt, his head tipped to

the side. "That so? And how are you gonna do that from behind those bars, Preacher? You gonna ask God to smite me?"

Being a former priest turned member of an MC, the jokes about God are something I get on the regular. Usually, they don't bother me a bit, but just hearing Alan say His name makes my skin crawl.

"I won't be behind these bars forever, asshole. And when I'm out, you're the first person I'm looking for. Your death will be slow, and you will be begging me to finish the job."

Alan's jaw ticks as I make my promise, his cold eyes hard and angry. His silence stretches on for far too long, and then he finally steps up to the bars, just far enough away that I can't reach him if I tried. "We're making our move on your club tomorrow. They don't have a fucking clue we're coming. You wanna hear our plan, Preacher?"

I don't move a muscle as I stare him down, helpless, but not willing to let him see my fear.

"We know where their clubhouse is now. We've been casing it for days. Your prospects don't do a very good job monitoring those gates."

Fucking idiot. He has no clue how much surveillance our club has surrounding our compound. My buddy Hashtag has that place under lock and key. Nobody's getting in without the club knowing well ahead of time.

"We're gonna draw them out, though. Make a statement."

Boo still hasn't moved from her place on the floor; she hasn't made a sound. Hasn't shed a tear. Not a flicker of life left in those gorgeous blue eyes.

"You're gonna help us do that, Preacher. You won't be alive for it, but when we drop your dead body at the front gate of that compound, the whole fucking club will gather to bring you in, and that's when we strike. We're gonna cut those fuckers down, right there at the gates. We'll shoot everything that fucking moves, and then, once we get inside, we'll find Big Dick's kid and his ol' lady, and bring them home. The plan is no survivors. Everyone dies. Women, children... even fucking dogs. Anything with a beating heart is going to meet their maker tomorrow night. So, I ask you, Preacher, how do you plan on killing me when you're already dead?"

I don't tell him the flaws in their stupid plan. I don't tell him that Hashtag likely already knows they're watching. I don't tell him that they'll never get a chance to surround the club. And I don't tell him that the Black Hoods would never fall for a childish ambush like that.

Instead, I tip my head to the side, shoving the rage in my veins as deep as it will go and smile. "You're a rapist and a fucking moron. I'll see you in hell, asshole, even if I have to escort you there myself."

The knowing grin on Alan's face falls as he stands taller and glares at me. I don't look away.

Rage brews in his eyes like a fire, and just when I think he's going to lunge for me, he turns and grabs Boo by the hair, dragging her to her feet.

Her naked body is limp, her feet barely moving as he forces her to stand. He doesn't approach the bars this time, but he wraps an arm around her waist, holding her to him and yanking her head back so her eyes are on me. The absence of awareness in them terrifies me more than anything.

"Boo, I will get you out of here," I tell her, my voice firm and loud. "I will save you from this sick fuck, but you need to stay with me."

Boo doesn't even seem to hear me, but Alan does.

"Fuck you," he roars, his face twisted with more hate and rage than I ever thought one human being could hold. "You want her so much? She'll die too. You just signed her fucking death warrant, motherfucker."

With one arm still around her waist, Alan steps away and drags Boo down the hall.

Panic and fear wash over me in a wave, nearly buckling my knees as I rush to the bars to peer around the corner, watching until they're out of my sight.

"Hold on, Boo!" I scream. "Just hold on. Don't let him fucking ruin you, baby. I will get you out of here!"

Just as I make that final promise, the heavy metal door at the end of the hall squeals and thumps closed with a heavy thud. Silence fills the air around me, draining the hope from my soul, leaving me powerless and filled with anguish.

BOO

A ROPE BITES into my wrists. I watch the scene around me as if I'm simply a spectator, observing Alan as he drags my body from the cells, my bare ass covered in his cum, and plops my limp body onto a metal chair, binding me there in the center of the main room. All eyes turn to watch as he tightens the rope, grunting and puffing with his effort.

"The fuck is this?" Big Dick asks, approaching just as Alan finishes tying my feet to the chair. "If this your new idea of foreplay, man, fuck. Do it somewhere else. I don't want to watch this shit."

"I do," one of the others says, laughing. "Can I make requests?"

"Fuck off, Bricker," Alan growls. "That's not what this is."

"Care to enlighten us, then? You've fucked her up

pretty good, man," someone else says. "If you don't want her anymore, I'll take her off your hands."

"Fuck off, all of you. She's mine. This isn't about her. It's the Black Hood." Alan pulls a bandana from his back pocket and stuffs it into my mouth. I gag at the intrusion of the filthy material, coming back to myself just enough to try to spit it out. Alan shoves it in even farther. "Spit that out, I'll break your fucking jaw," he orders, his finger in my face.

I know I should be afraid. This is likely the end for me, and for Priest. I should be terrified, fighting back, even, but I can't. I can't even muster up enough energy to struggle against my bindings.

Alan's going to tell them about my phone call the other day. But why? What benefit does it have for him now? He's got everything he wants. My spirit has finally been broken, and Priest is about to die. If he tells Big Dick about that phone call, it's not only my ass on the line, but his as well for breaking club rules.

Big Dick looks on curiously. "Explain."

"Boo here made a friend in the cells," Alan informs him, turning his attention to him and the others. "You wanted leverage against that big bastard, and I fucking found it. It's her." Alan grabs my hair and yanks my head back. "You should've seen him. He was begging for me to stop fucking with her. She's our ticket. We just have to punch it at the right time."

Hot tears roll down my face as I come back to my body. This is really it. The end. There's no way out of this. My resolve to stay alive is completely broken now. Priest's voice repeating "I'm sorry" plays in my head like a broken record. Having him as an audience hadn't stopped Alan. It had empowered him, and in doing so, stole what was left of my dignity, and the power I'd only recently found out I had. It's all gone.

"We don't need leverage," Big Dick says, circling me like a Hyena playing with its prey, a deep frown wrinkling his face. "We have a plan. We know where the kid is. The preacher dies tomorrow and we move in. So, what's your game here? You know we can't kill this one."

"We don't have to kill her to break him. He just has to think we did."

Big Dick frowns. "Again, I ask why. He's dying tomorrow."

"Because that fucker thinks he can get out of here. He thinks he has some sort of claim on my fucking bitch. Because he's a Black Hood, and I want to make him squirm. I want to break that son of a bitch before he dies."

Big Dick studies Alan for several seconds before nodding. "Why not? We got nothin' going on tonight. Messing with the preacher might be fun. So, you want him to think what? That you killed her?"

"I want him to hear her screams," Alan acknowledges, his voice a deep growl.

His eyes are dark. Darker than I've ever seen them before. Alan has put me through hell many times over the years, but he's never looked as evil as he does right now. A cold chill creeps into my bones, sending shivers along my spine as I peer up at him in fear.

Big Dick stares at Alan a moment longer, mulling over his cruel words. *Please, God. Please, don't let them do this.*

A cruel smile spreads across Big Dick's face and he moves, pulling a long knife with a curved tip from the holster at his belt. The sharp edge of the blade gleams under the canister lights above as he runs his thumb across it, drawing blood. It's razor sharp.

Any hope I might've had that Big Dick would put an end to this crazy assault evaporates as he approaches, twirling that knife in his hand before stopping with the tip barely touching my nose. I suck in a ragged breath, choking on the bandana in my mouth. With his free hand, Big Dick grabs the bandana and jerks it out.

"Please, don't do this," I plead, my voice cracking. "I don't mean anything to him."

Alan shifts forward, coming up next to Big Dick, and glares down at me. "You're lying. A man doesn't fight like that unless you mean something. You fucked him, didn't you?"

"No!" I gasp.

"I could cut that pretty little throat of yours right now," Big Dick says, the knife dropping to press against my neck while studying me from his position. "What has he told you, Boo? He tell you about my son?"

"No," I sob. "You did. You all fucking did. Just because I'm your prisoner, doesn't mean I don't hear what's going on around here."

"Must not be keeping her satisfied, Alan," a voice says from somewhere else in the room. "Not if she has time to listen."

"Should've let me have her," another says. "My cock in her mouth would keep her busy."

"I'll kill you where you fucking stand, Bricker," Alan snarls. "Prospect, go get the new girl." His body thrums with evil energy, trembling from his place beside Big Dick. He has a plan. Another shiver ripples down my spine, settling in my stomach.

The prospect disappears down the hall. The thud of a door being kicked follows, and then the blood-curdling sound of several feminine screams. Heavy footfalls approach as the screams grow louder, and then he returns, dragging a girl I don't recognize by her long black hair. She's young. Barely legal, if I were to guess. Maybe not even that.

"What do you want me to do with this one?" he asks, stopping just inches away.

The girl's fearful eyes meet mine, growing wide when she takes in the state of me. Her sobs grow louder.

"Tie her up and put her outside the hallway. Let's give Boo's friend a better seat for the show."

The prospect complies, moving to the chair by the door. The woman scans the room, pleading with anyone that will listen. "Help me. Please, help!"

The men ignore her pleas, all of them watching as the prospect ties her to the chair. They don't care what happens now. Girls like her—like me—we're like livestock to them, and they're about to put her down.

"Wait!" I beg. "Why her? Why not me? I'm the one you're mad at. Hurt me. Kill me!"

Big Dick releases his knife at my throat and leans down to whisper in my ear. "I can't kill you, sweetheart." He points his knife at the girl in the chair. "But I can kill her."

"No, please," I continue to beg, choking on the sobs in my throat, barely able to breathe. "She's just a child. She's innocent."

"No one who comes through these doors is innocent, Boo. You, of all people, should know that."

"Just kill me!" I cry. "I'm the one you want."

"Oh, little Boo. We have other plans for you. You're going to make me one rich son of a bitch, baby. I'm not letting that slip through my fingers by getting careless now. Not when I'm so close to my payday."

My uncle sent me here years ago. There's not a snow-ball's chance in hell of him having the money to pay them back for whatever debt that's owed, plus thirteen years of interest on top of it. They'll never get paid for me. We'd lived in a single wide trailer that should've been condemned before I was even born. My uncle has nothing, let alone the amount they're hoping to get from him.

"Do it," he orders, turning his gaze to me. Bricker and Alan stalk toward the girl who watches them through wide eyes, her entire body trembling with fear. "Watch her bleed for you, Boo," Big Dick sneers, his lips brushing against my ear. "Her death is on your hands."

He shifts away as the girl's screams fill the room, piercing my ears and my already broken heart. Alan steps forward, his fist flying toward her, landing against her face with a sickening thud of bone on flesh. Blood instantly fills her mouth and trickles down her chin.

The poor girl sobs, her pleas muffled around her tattered lips. Alan brandishes a knife and grins back at me, his face twisted with some sort of sick pride as he plunges the blade into the soft flesh of her belly.

"No!" I cry. "No, please! Stop!"

Alan laughs. "Scream for me, Boo. Show your friend in there how we treat women who break the fucking rules."

And I do. My voice joins the girl's, both of us

screaming at the top of our lungs, pleading for them to stop. Our cries mingle together, bouncing off the walls and landing on the ears of the men in the room, none of which will ever lift a finger to save us.

"You hear that, motherfucker?" Alan calls down the hallway toward Priest. I can hear the clanging and banging from here. Priest is going crazy down there. "This is because of you, asshole. She'll die because of you."

Alan pulls his gun from his belt holster and presses the barrel against her forehead. The girl sobs, her eyes focused on mine. We cry together, locked in the knowledge that her end is coming soon.

"Too bad you have to die," he says, glowering down at the crying girl. "You look like you would've been fun to break."

"No!" I scream, my heart hammering against my chest as I try to free myself from the ropes.

Down the hall, Priest is screaming my name, the sound of his assault on the bars echoing down the hall. He screams my name over and over again, promising death to Alan and the others.

Alan grins and locks his eyes on me as he cocks back the hammer and presses the barrel deeper into the girl's forehead.

Just then, the door from outside slams open, and the prospect that had always shown me some kindness comes barreling inside. Prez," he gasps, hauling in air like he'd just run a marathon. "We have company."

Big Dick frowns. "The fuck—"

His question is cut off as the prospect's head reels back, blood and bone spraying from the side of it before he drops to his knees. We barely have a chance to process what's happening before the men pour inside the door, guns drawn, their faces filled with pure rage.

The Black Hoods. They're here.

Chapter 15

PRIEST

THE SOUND of the gunshot coming from far off in the main room hits my ears like the bullet itself, shattering my heart and my hope. He shot her. He fucking shot Boo, and it's my fault. I brought her into this. I asked her to help me, knowing full well that she was in just as much danger as I was.

And now she's dead.

I fall back away from the bars, my hands battered and bloodied from punching and pulling on them in my desperation to get to Boo. My back hits the far wall and I sink to the floor, my head in my hands, ignoring the yelling and screaming now coming from the other room.

None of it matters now. Boo is dead, and soon, I will be too, and I deserve to be. As much as I don't deserve to die here at the Screwballs' hands, I do deserve to die after putting Boo in danger. My death is inevitable. I just hope they stop their arguing down there and hurry the fuck up, because my soul is ripping to shreds as I think about the pink-haired girl and how brave she's been to survive in this place, and all for nothing.

Another gunshot rings through the air, but I'm too deep in my sorrow to give a shit. And then another, and another. Three more gunshots follow.

I pause in my self-torture and frown. Why so many shots? Surely Boo was taken out with the first one. And if that hadn't worked, only one more would've been sufficient.

Lifting my head, I strain my ears, hoping to catch the words coming from behind the closed door at the end of the long hall. Shouts and screams continue, but I can't make out the words.

When I hear the door slam open, followed by heavy footsteps approaching, I clamor to my feet and rush over to the bars, ready to die, but not about to take my death sitting down. I'll look these fuckers in the eyes as they take me out. I'll haunt their fucking memories until their dying breath.

When the first man comes into view, I'm fully expecting to see Big Dick, or even Alan. Instead, it's Judge who comes to the front of my cell, the heavy metal key already in his hand.

"You ready to come home, asshole?" he asks, a hint of a smirk on his lips.

Relief hits me like a brick wall, knocking the air from my lungs as I stare back at him through the bars. I have no words. Less than a second ago, I was waiting to die, and now that the cavalry is here, I'm frozen in place.

Judge puts the key in the lock, releasing the door with a heavy metal thunk. "Jesus, look at you," he mutters as he slides the door out of the way and steps inside. "These assholes really fucked you up."

"Boo," I say, staring into Judge's eyes, knowing I'm not making any sense.

Judge frowns. "What?"

I shake my head, frustrated, because I know I sound like a fucking moron, but I don't have time to explain. Pushing past Judge, I move down the hallway to the door, hobbling as I go, ignoring the stabbing pain tearing through my entire body.

Judge doesn't ask any more questions. Without a word, he follows me, a gun in his hand, ready to fire as I approach the open door. Through it, I can see a girl in a chair, slumped to the side, tears streaming down her face, but it's not Boo.

Stepping out into the main room, my gaze skips over the three men lying on the floor. One dead, and the others with their hands on the back of their heads with StoneFace towering over them, the barrel of his gun moving from one to the other, a wordless threat that he will absolutely blow them away if they move so much as an inch.

A flash of pink catches my eye, the only hint of beauty in this place. Moving faster than my broken body should, I approach, my heart a motionless rock in my chest. She's tied to a chair that's been tipped to the side. Her eyes are closed, her mouth open in a silent scream. Blood trickles from her head, the line snaking across her forehead and over her nose, before joining the small pool on the floor beneath her.

As I reach her, I crouch, taking her chin in my hands. "Boo! Boo! Baby, wake up. Boo?"

She doesn't respond. Her hands are bound at the wrist behind the chair, and her ankles are tethered to the front legs, which has toppled to the side with her, it's unconscious prisoner.

"Knife!" I shout, my bloody and swollen fingers working at the knots. "I need a fucking knife!"

TK steps forward, a buck knife in his outstretched hand. He looks worried as I snatch it, and begin frantically sawing away at the thick ropes.

"Boo!" I call, the rope tearing free one tiny thread at a time. "Fuck. Somebody help me!"

The chatter in the room falls silent as the others draw closer.

"Here, man. Let me." StoneFace kneels down beside

me and places his hand on mine, pausing my struggle with the rope.

I hand him the knife, but I don't take my eyes off of Boo's face as he frees her body from the chair. As soon as she's free, I fall to the floor and pull her into my lap, covering her naked body the best I can while cradling her like an infant. The blood is coming from a gash just above her hairline, the edges of the wound singed. A bullet graze.

"Boo," I say, turning her face toward me.

"Is she breathing?" StoneFace asks, moving to kneel in front of us, his fingers moving to her wrist to feel for a pulse.

"I don't know," I whisper. "I don't know."

"She's got a pulse." Moving away, he gives us space. "A strong one. Looks like she's just passed out."

Relieved, I bury my face in her neck, inhaling the scent of her for the first time. She smells of blood and sweat, and a hint of strawberries. She's alive. Alan didn't kill her after all. The fucker didn't have time.

"That the girl who called me?" Judge asks, his voice low.

I nod, not moving my face from her neck. "Her name is Boo," I tell him. "She fucking saved me."

Silence follows my sentence, and then Judge places a hand on my shoulder. "Then let's get her home."

"Okay." Pain and exhaustion wash over me as I hold

her closer. "You did it, Boo. You fucking did it. We're getting out of here."

Several moments pass before StoneFace returns with a blanket to wrap her in. "Let me take her, man. You can sit with her in the van, but we gotta get you both out of here and to the doc."

Helpless, I watch as he covers her up, scoops her into his arms, and carries her toward the door. My body doesn't even have the energy to follow. All I want to do is curl up right here and go to sleep.

Sleep and Boo. Fuck. Her monitoring bracelet is still on. The last thing we need is for those fuckers to have a beacon to track her down. We can't leave with that still on her.

"Wait!" I call out just before StoneFace is gone. "She has an ankle monitor on. One of the guys can track it. We need to remove it."

StoneFace nods. "I saw it. I'll have Hash get it off before we leave. No one will know where she is."

"Let's go." Taking my hand, TK helps me up off the floor. When my knees threaten to give out, he wraps his arm around my waist and holds me up.

"What do you want me to do with these fuckers?" Hashtag inquires, standing over two of the Screwballs still kneeling on the floor, watching everything going down.

Judge turns and spits on the floor in their direction. "Kill them."

I squint against the sun when we step out of the building. Being locked in a dark room for several days has made my eyes sensitive to the big ball of fire hovering in the sky. "Big Dick," I say to TK. "He wants Harrison."

TK's jaw grows hard. "I know. He and a bunch of the others took off out the back when we barged in. Fuckers had their guns out. One of them shot GP, but he's all right. Just grazed."

I pause and meet his gaze. "They got away?"

"For now."

"Why didn't you follow them? They're after your woman and her kid."

TK clenches his jaw, but it's Judge who answers for him. "We were here for you. We got one girl stabbed and bleeding out. Your girl isn't even conscious, and you look like you've been fed to a fucking meat grinder. Let's deal with one thing at a time."

"But Cora—"

"Cora and Harrison are safe," he assures me. "That fucker won't get to them before we put him and the rest of his club down."

I don't know if that will happen, but the fact that Cora and the boy are safe is reassuring enough to push me forward.

TK helps me into the back of the utility van. There are no seats back here, so I climb in and settle against the side wall. The unconscious woman from the main room is curled up on a blanket on the floor, a bright bloom of blood staining her pink cotton shirt.

As I take Boo from StoneFace and settle her head in my lap, I make a promise to her and to myself. I will end each and every one of those fuckers. But first, I need to take care of my girl.

Chapter 16

BOO

THEY SAY WHEN YOU DIE, a white light and the past flashes before your eyes. I certainly saw a white light, but it was soon replaced with darkness. Cool darkness and peace.

It's funny, this peace. I'd wished for it for so long, but now that it's here, I don't know how to accept it. It feels unreal. Am I dead? That's what I had wanted, but now I don't know what to do with it. The afterlife is certainly not the same as the descriptions in the bible. There's no golden gate, no angels, no mansions, and no streets of gold. Just darkness.

Shit. Is this hell? Maybe. But if it is, this would still be a better life than the one I had before.

Peace and quiet. I float in the darkness, my mind blinking in and out. I'm weightless. There's no pain.

Something rattles near me. *What is that?*

Whatever it is, I can't see it, but I know it's there. Engulfed in the darkness, I lift my arms, feeling the space around me until I find something hard. Something warm and alive.

But how? How can I have arms to feel? How does something feel alive? I'm dead, *aren't I?*

My head spins, a headache beginning at the front of my skull. The pain gets stronger with every beat of my heart. A drumline of thuds. *Kah-thunk. Kah-thunk.*

My heart? My heartbeat? Oh, God, I'm alive? Like, really alive?

The light I'd seen flashes ahead of me, blinking in and out of existence until it flashes so brightly, I curl into myself. It finally gives way, and my eyes open.

Well, shit. I'm alive.

I recoil in pain. Suddenly, as my mind discovers I'm still among the living, so does my entire body. Aches reach every cell I'm made of. I'm afraid to move, but I have to. I can't lie here forever.

One by one, I will my muscles to move. I start with my little toe, then I wiggle my feet. It hurts so bad, but I keep going, moving my legs and my knees, then my hip. It's as if my entire body is rebooting.

"Fuck," I groan.

Everything hurts. Absolutely everything. Even my hair follicles.

Peeling my eyelids open, I blink and squint against the light.

It takes a few seconds for my vision to finally clear. Okay, this is not hell, but where the hell am I?

I've never seen this room before. It's small. The walls are bare and stark white. No photos. No posters. Nothing. *Oh, fuck.*

I crane my neck, ignoring the way it cracks in the process, and notice a small desk near a wooden door. With a shift of my shoulder, I inch myself up. The softness cradling me is a bed. A mattress that has to be the closest thing to Heaven I'd ever felt. My fingers splay across the soft black sheets.

A soft snore comes from behind me.

I'm not alone.

My body reacts before I even realize what I'm doing. Shooting from the bed, I stumble on unsteady legs, wobbling until my knees hit the carpet. I don't dare look back. My fight or flight response has taken over. With no fight left in me, I can only run. Run and pray that what I find on the other side of that door isn't the Screwballs, or any of their associates. On all fours, I crawl toward it. My blood thrums inside my throbbing head with each move I make. Reaching up, I take the doorknob in my hand, surprised to find it unlocked when I turn it.

"Boo?" A voice calls out from behind me. "It's okay. You're okay." Two arms curl around my waist, pulling me into a warm embrace. A hard chest presses flat against my back as I freeze in terror. "Boo, baby, it's me. Look at me, honey. You're safe."

Priest's voice is soft and warm, but I shake my head, not willing to be fooled. "This isn't real. It's a dream, or a vision. You're dead. I'm dead."

"Shh," he whispers in my ear, rocking my body gently as his nose presses to the crook of my neck. "You're not dead, sweetheart, and neither am I. You saved us, honey. You called Judge, and you fucking saved us."

I shift, my muscles screaming, but I need to see him. I need to know this is real.

Priest's soft eyes stare down at me. His wounds are fresh, but bandages and stitches replace the blood he'd been covered in since the day I first saw him. But it's him. A cleaned-up version of the man in the cells. My friend.

"I promise, honey, this is all real."

I stare at him for far too long before asking, "Where are we?"

"My room at our clubhouse."

"Your clubhouse," I say, repeating his words back to him.

They came. I didn't imagine it. The Black Hoods really came to save us.

"We're safe." I've never said those two exact words together in a sentence before. "You're sure?"

Priest nods and turns my body to face him. "As safe as we can be, sweetheart. This place is locked down tight. No one is getting in here."

The smile that takes over my face catches us both off guard. A smile. A genuine smile. When was the last time I'd done that?

I watch as Priest's lips turn up at the corners, and then I laugh. But my laughter doesn't last long. Instead, it morphs into a sob before I can stop it, and then uncontrollable sobs erupt from inside of me.

Priest's arms pull me to him, cradling me against his chest. He doesn't utter a word until every tear escapes my body. He holds me, providing comfort and understanding, and most importantly, safety.

"I know, baby, I know," he coos, rubbing his hands up and down my arms. "Come back to bed. You need rest. We both do."

"I shouldn't be in your room. Is there another room for the women?"

"Women?" Frowning, Priest places a finger under my chin and tips my head back so I'm looking up at him. "Boo, I told you, we aren't like them."

"So why am I in here?" I hate to ask the question, but if I've learned anything during my time on this earth, it's that men only want something from you, and usually that something is sex. Before, Priest had wanted my help, but now that he no longer needs it, I know what he expects.

"If I had to take a guess, the guys put you in here with me. After seeing the doc, I passed the fuck out. But they knew it would be better for you to wake up next to someone you know than in a strange room, especially considering..." he trails off. He saw firsthand what happened to me there, but it appears he can't bring himself to say it out loud.

His explanation makes sense, but still, I'm in no condition to provide him with any comfort. My head is throbbing, my body aches, and my eyelids feel like they weigh ten pounds each. With a nod, I slowly look around the room. "I can sleep on the floor, I guess."

"You're not sleeping on the floor," he mutters, leading me back to the bed. "The bed is fine. If one of us is sleeping on the floor, it's going to be me. But I'd rather not, considering the hell I've been through. If that makes you feel better, though, I will." He shifts away from me, turning my body and lowering me onto the bed. Once I'm settled, he tucks me in and takes a step back. It's then that I get a better look at him.

Priest's shirtless upper body is covered in tattoos. An ornate cross takes up the muscled expanse of his chest, contrasting against his dark olive skin. His abs... God, his abs. Like chiseled marble on a statue. His shoulders are bandaged, but the swirl of tattoos peek out from beneath them. His muscular legs are wrapped in white bandages. He smiles when he catches me staring at him.

"Go to sleep, honey. You can ogle me once we've rested."

"I'm not ogling you," I huff, heat rising to my cheeks. "I just…"

"You what, Boo?"

I've just never seen a man as massive as he is. He's like a giant work of art. The man God made for all other men to strive to be like. He's handsome and tanned, and has the face of an avenging angel. He's perfection. But as tired as I am, I'm not about to tell him that.

"Never mind," I say with a shake of my head. Hoping he'll change the subject, I snuggle down deeper into the blankets and yawn. "It's not important."

Priest smirks, but he doesn't push it. "So where am I sleeping, honey? Because my legs are about to give out, and I need a place to crash."

Biting my lip, I stare up at his glorious, yet battered body. Priest has never done anything to make me feel uncomfortable. He's never made lewd comments, or put his hands on me to cause me pain. Maybe he's right. Maybe he is different from the Screwballs.

"I'll take the floor," he concludes, reaching for his pillow.

"No." Pushing up from the bed, I reach out for his hand. Slowly, I grab the blankets on the other side and draw them back. "Sleep here. It's okay with me if it's okay with you."

I watch him as he considers this. I don't know what he's thinking, but he must agree, because he drops his pillow back on the bed next to me and climbs in.

The bed jostles as he adjusts himself, hissing a curse through his teeth as he moves. Finally, he settles, and neither of us speak as we lie side by side, both of us soaking up the silence.

My mind whirls with questions, but only one seems important right now. The one question only he can answer for me.

Rolling to my side, I face him with my hands resting beneath my cheek. "What happened to them, to the Screwballs? Are they dead?"

Sighing, Priest reaches for my hand. "I wish I could say they were, but they're not. Not all of them, anyway. But the rest is a conversation for tomorrow. We need to sleep." He gives my hand a squeeze and smiles. "Close your eyes, baby. I promise to not hog the blankets."

I watch his eyes close, his hand still holding mine. Alan did that in bed sometimes, but when he did it, it was to keep me there, to hold me prisoner. But when Priest does it, it's tender and affectionate. Soothing.

His face grows slack as I study him, and his breaths

come out in slow, steady puffs. I don't know how long I watch him sleep before exhaustion finally takes hold. I sink my head down into the fluffy pillow, and allow the sound of his soft snores to carry me into a much-needed sleep.

PRIEST

"ALAN, PLEASE... NO!"

The pained scream rips through my throat and past my lips, forcing me out of bed in an instant. I snatch up the Glock I keep in the drawer of my nightstand before I've even looked to see what's happening.

I turn, gun raised, and scan the room.

Nothing.

There's no hidden threat. No Alan. No Screwballs. Just nothing. Except, that's not entirely true. There's Boo.

Curled up in the fetal position at the foot of my bed, Boo's sleeping form trembles as whimpers escape her pouting lips. Her feet kick out just a little as she dreams. God, I can't imagine what this woman has been through. Well, I can, actually. I'd seen it firsthand, but I'd only seen it over a period of a few days. Boo had been with the Screwballs since she was just a child.

The idea of any of them fuckers touching her as a child sets off a deep rage that can be felt in my bones. It's common among a sane population to hate pedophiles, but my own experiences have turned that hate into something vaster, something murderous.

The memory of his black suit and white collar floats through my mind before I can stop it. I try so hard to shove memories of him down so deep, they have no chance of resurfacing. But Boo's horrors bring them all to the surface.

The way he walked. The way he smelled. The way he groomed me into believing that he was my friend.

I'd grown up in a Catholic home. My father had left when I was just a young child, taking off with a woman he'd met at work. This left my mother struggling to make ends meet, so we had moved in with my Gran.

Gran was a wonderful woman, full of love, and a wonderful baker. And nobody loved the church like my Gran.

Mom had worked a lot back then, busting her ass to make enough money to keep clothes on our backs and a roof over our heads. I loved her dearly, but our relationship wasn't nearly as close as the one I'd had with Gran.

She taught me to cook and to do laundry. She had freshly baked cookies out on warming trays when I came home from school each day. Gran helped me with my homework, and volunteered at my school. She even taught me how to waltz when I was just ten years old.

Going to Mass was an integral part of our lives. We went every Wednesday and Saturday evenings, as well as Sunday mornings. On Thursday's, we went to confession, and then volunteered in the kitchen, handing out meals to the cities less fortunate. It was the Lord's work. At least, that's what my Gran believed, and since my Gran was the smartest person I knew, I'd believed it too.

As soon as I'd turned ten, my Gran had decided it was time for me to serve the church in yet another way, and she made sure I went through all the steps to become an altar boy. It wasn't a job I loved or hated, but it made her proud, which made me proud to do it.

Father Gibson was the acting priest at that time, and he'd taken an active role in the lives of his altar boys. He taught us lessons from the bible, and made sure we were well practiced in our roles. A couple of times, he had taken all of us camping at a lake just outside of the city, where we fished, hiked, and swam all day.

It was just after getting back from one of those camping trips that my wholesome life was shattered.

Gran was due to pick me up, but she was running late. The other boys were long gone, and I was still at the church with all my camping gear half an hour later.

"I'm sure she'll be along soon, son," Father Gibson

had said. "Why don't you come back to my office and I'll get you something to drink while you wait."

But it wasn't a drink he had given me.

"It's okay, Mateo," he had whispered into my ear as he stole my innocence. "Just relax, and see how good it feels."

It hadn't felt good. Not during the moment when he'd raped me, and not any moment since when the memory of what he'd done that afternoon crept back in.

I told my Gran what had happened the moment I'd gotten into her car. She could tell right away that something was bothering me. Though Father Gibson was adamant that it remain a secret between us, I couldn't keep it to myself.

My Gran might've been an old woman, but she was a hellcat when you fucked with her family. She had marched right into that church and called Father Gibson out on what he'd done. The police were notified, and he'd been hauled away. I never saw him again, and Gran had assured me that I never would.

I'd spent the rest of my youth acting as altar boy for the priest that had come to take Father Gibson's place. Father Rafferty was a much older man, but he was fair, and he kept his hands to himself. That was all I'd ever wanted.

Becoming a priest myself was never really a life goal,

but as I grew up, I'd realized how much the church was there to help people. I had a strong belief in God, and I wanted to be the one to get people excited about their faith.

I would've been a good priest too, but I never made it to the end of seminary school. During my final semester, I had walked in on a well-loved Bishop while he was molesting a young boy. My faith had snapped in that moment. It wasn't just Father Gibson that was a bad egg. Here was another man—a Bishop, for fuck's sake—doing the same sick shit to yet another child.

I'd gone straight to the archbishop right after helping that boy back to his home. The archbishop had nodded, his face grave and concerned. He'd assured me that he would handle it, but when I'd come in the next day, the bishop was walking out with his suitcase in hand.

The archbishop had told him about my report, and had given the sick bastard a slap on the wrist, assigning him to a church in a different state. There was no punishment. There was no reporting it to the police. It was simply swept under the rug, with the expectation it would never be spoken of again.

My Gran had long since passed on, but I believed then, as I do now, that she would've understood why I had dropped out. Hell, she would've helped me pack.

How was I expected to devote my life to a God, whose worshipping leaders turned out to be such vile human beings? If God were real, how could he allow it to happen over and over again?

Teeth chattering, Boo groans in pain. Finally, I'm no longer engulfed in my blackest memories, but back here with her. And she needs me.

Placing the Glock back in my nightstand, I hobble around to the other side of the bed. My body screams in protest as I lift her from the end and shift her body up the mattress, resting her head gently onto the pillow.

Her eyelids flutter as I tuck the blankets around her once more, noting that her skin feels ice-cold.

"What's happening?" she questions, struggling to open her eyes.

"It's okay, honey. You were just having a bad dream."

My answer seems to get through to her, because she stops struggling to wake up and rolls onto her side, her hand reaching across to where I had just been. "Come lay with me?" she murmurs. "Please?"

Her question cools that pit of anger I'd been stewing in. And how can I say no to this sweet woman? Rounding the bed, I slip back under the covers and pull her against my body.

I wrap my arms around her, and she rests her head against my chest. It hurts like a bitch, thanks to a few broken ribs, but I don't give a fuck. I want her close... I *need* her close.

"Thank you, Priest."

Slowly, gently, I press my lips to the top of her head. "Sleep, Angel."

Chapter 18

BOO

I DON'T THINK I've ever gotten this much sleep in my entire life. To be honest, I can't remember a single instance where I've slept more than a few hours, but those had been spread out over days. Sleep has never come easy to me, but here, the second my head hits the pillow, I drift off.

Could it be the pain medicine the club doctor gave me? Sure. Or maybe it's the giant man sleeping next to me? Also possible. I just know that my body likes the rest it's gotten. I'd barely left the bed outside of trips to the en suite bathroom in Priest's room, and to snack on whatever someone had left for us to eat. Priest has barely moved, either. His injuries were far worse than mine, according to the conversation I'd overheard with the doctor, who had sequestered Priest to the bathroom to change his bandages. The Screwballs didn't hold back on him. Neither of us had fared well, but he'd bored the brunt of their violence.

With a long stretch of my arms, I pull the blanket away from my body. A slick film of sweat covers my arms. Priest's body is like an oven when he sleeps. Though, I won't complain about that. It was nice to be warm for once.

I stretch again, but this time, I catch a whiff of myself. *Jesus, I need a shower. I seriously reek.*

Peering over my shoulder, I find Priest's side of the bed empty, and a jolt of panic pierces my chest. Where did he go? Did he leave me here?

Relax, Boo. You're safe. Priest would never let anything happen to you.

With a deep, cleansing breath, I place my feet on the floor and force my stiff body to stand. My muscles creak and complain at the movement. I need a hot shower.

Shit. I don't have any clothes.

I look down at what I'm wearing. A pair of snug, pink flannel shorts, and an oversized T-shirt with a picture of the Pope flipping the bird.

Just then, the bathroom door swings open and Priest steps out, the steam from the shower billowing around him like a cloud. My mouth goes dry as I take in his wet hair, as well as the water dripping onto his chest and trickling down his abs in long, winding streaks.

The black towel slung low across his hips showcases

the muscular V of his lower abdomen, dipping beneath the edge. Unable to look away, my eyes trail farther south, and I shiver when I see the outline of his cock pressing against the thin material.

Jesus, Mary, and Joseph. How was this man a priest looking like that?

"Morning," he greets me with a wide smile. I continue to stare as he runs a second towel through his hair, messing with his long locks, making him look rumpled, and somehow, even more gorgeous. A flutter erupts low in my belly, and my cheeks grow hot.

"I uh… Morning." *Real smooth, idiot.*

I will my eyes to look away, but it's like they're permanently stuck on the man in front of me drying his hair in slow motion. I would swear he's doing it on purpose just to unnerve me. But that couldn't be, could it?

"Sleep okay?"

"Yeah, fine," I mumble.

"Shower's still running if you wanna get cleaned up. There are extra towels under the sink." When I don't respond, he asks, "Boo, you sure you're okay?"

I clear my throat, my eyes still glued to the bulge under the towel. "Yes, I'm fine. Perfectly fine."

His lips turn up in a knowing smirk. "If you say so." He tosses the towel he used for his hair into a hamper near the bathroom door, but makes no attempt to move. "Nice shirt, by the way."

I peer down at it again, my fingers tugging at the hem. "Yeah, about that… I know I didn't come here in any clothes. When your club showed up, I was—"

"In bad shape," he interjects gently. "We wrapped you up in a blanket and brought you here. And in case you're wondering, I believe it was Blair who brought you the shorts."

"And the shirt?"

"Oh, that's mine. One of my favorites." He laughs. "Actually, it was the first thing I bought when I left the church."

My eyes grow wide. I can't keep the surprise out of my voice when I ask, "You bought this? Wouldn't that go against the whole religious thing?"

He shrugs. "Probably."

I consider that, but not for long. I remember how terrible I smell, and I bet I look even worse. Though, I am curious… "You still owe me the story on that, by the way."

"I do. How about I tell you after you get cleaned up. I'll grab you a fresh set of clothes and see what's left in the kitchen. It's Saturday, so the ladies should have gone all out. Anything you'd like in particular?"

"Surprise me." And it will be a surprise, seeing as I'd

never been given a choice of what I wanted to eat. The club chose for me.

"I can do that." He tips his head to the side. "Think you're up to eating with the club today? Meet some of the guys and the ladies?"

The thought of meeting everyone makes me feel a little uneasy, but I say, "Okay."

"No pressure, Boo. None." His gaze lingers on my face. "How about I bring the food up and we can eat in here. You'll meet everyone soon enough."

He moves away from the door, and I make my way inside. The scent of his body wash lingers between us, a mix of sandalwood and spice. The same scent I'd smelled on his sheets.

"I'll be back with food and clothes."

As soon as the latch clicks and I'm completely alone inside, I rest my forehead on the wood separating us, listening to his footsteps as he moves about the room. When the clunking of his boots on the floor can't be heard anymore, I turn toward the mirror. The steam from the hot shower has fogged it up, which is probably for the best. I don't know what I look like right now, and I don't want to.

Stripping away my borrowed clothes, I fold them neatly and lay them on the counter by the sink. Pulling back the shower curtain, I step inside, hissing when the hot spray hits my skin, stinging every wound on my body. Cursing, I plaster myself to the tile wall while fumbling with the handle, trying to adjust the temperature. After a few seconds, I stick my hand out and test the water.

So much better.

I tip my head back and moan as the stream rolls over my aching muscles, melting away the tension. It's not until I look down that I see just what a mess I'd been. The water circling down the drain at my feet is pink from the blood, mixed with dirt and other filth. *Gross.*

Spying a bottle of Priest's body wash, I squirt some into my hands. The smell brings me a surprising amount of comfort as I lather up and run it over my skin. Though I like the idea of smelling like him, I can't help but wonder what kind of life he leads here with his club. I notice the lack of feminine shower products, so there's either no particular woman in his life, or there's a rotation of them. I don't believe for a second I'm the first woman to shower in Priest's room.

He probably fucks them in their rooms. This is his place, his sanctuary. Women don't belong in here. The hateful thoughts assault my mind in Alan's voice, causing my blood to run cold.

"No," I growl low, angry that Alan's abuse is so ingrained in my psyche, it even reaches me here, in a place he has no business being.

A soft tapping on the door pulls me out of my manic thoughts. "You okay?"

"Fine," I call out over the splashing water.

"I have your clothes. I'll put them on the counter."

"Sounds good. Thank you."

Doing a second wash of my hair, I do one last thorough wash of my skin, and when the water finally runs clear, only then do I turn off the water and step out.

Making quick work of drying off, I pick up the shorts. They're similar to the ones I had woken up in, with cutouts running along the sides. The T-shirt is huge, and I can't help but giggle at the black cat with devil horns under the name *Luci-Purr*. It's like he's on a mission to rib God.

Slipping on the clothes, I take the toothbrush Priest had left, out of the wrapper, and scrub my teeth until they look like they've been polished. I also find a hairbrush in a drawer under the sink. I look somewhat presentable when I finish, but for some reason, I feel nervous about leaving the bathroom. It's the first time I've ever felt safe doing things as simple as showering, dressing, even brushing my teeth.

Taking a deep breath, I reach for the handle and step out into the bedroom. Priest is nowhere to be found, but there's a plate of food loaded with bacon, eggs, and hash browns. A feast that could easily have fed me for a week. Next to it sits a glass of water and two white pills.

Mouthwatering, I settle down on the bed and tear into the crispy bacon, which is cooked to perfection. The second it hits my tongue, I moan in appreciation.

"Damn. If I'd have known bacon would make you sound like that, I'd have gotten you more," Priest quips, stepping into the room with a full plate in his hand.

Cheeks burning from embarrassment, I mumble, "Sorry," as I drop the bacon back onto the plate.

"Don't be." He takes a seat across from me. "I imagine this is your first decent meal in a while?"

If he only knew. For years, I've had to fight for every scrap I've eaten. I don't tell him that, though. Instead, I stuff a forkful of eggs into my mouth.

Everything tastes amazing. My stomach is so thankful to finally be filled with actual food, it growls.

"Slow down, Angel. You haven't eaten much in a while. You're gonna make yourself sick."

I pause, fork at my lips, and look down at my plate. He hasn't even touched his plate yet, and mine is almost empty. "Sorry."

"Stop saying you're sorry. Nothin' to be sorry for." He offers me two strips of his bacon. "Here."

"I can't take your food," I exclaim. "Patches eat first."

Frowning, he reaches forward and places the bacon onto my plate. "No. We eat together."

I don't argue, because I am still hungry. He leans back and starts to eat, and after a moment, I join him. When we're both finished, he reaches over, takes my plate, and sets them both on the nightstand.

"Doc sent some more painkillers if you want them."

I shake my head. I need to keep my wits about me until I have a better lay of the land here. Drugging myself isn't an option. Not until I know for sure that I can trust these men. Clear heads stay alive. Clear heads stay safe.

Though Priest has reassured me multiple times, I still don't know how I feel about being here. Aside from Priest, the only other person I've seen is the doc, and he's not even an actual part of the club.

Is Priest intentionally keeping them away? Had he staked his claim on me like Alan had? The thought of another Alan churns my full stomach.

Think of anything else. Anything. Don't waste the food you've been given by puking.

But, why am I here? I've asked myself that question a dozen times between my naps. Maybe more. The Black Hoods didn't have to save me. I meant nothing to them, but yet, here I am. Safe under Priest's care. But why me? Why save me and not the others?

Finally, I force myself to look him in the eye and ask, "Why did you save me?"

Priest blinks, burrowing his brow in confusion. "Why wouldn't I save you?"

"Because I'm not worth saving."

"Fuck that," he growls, taking my hand. "Boo, without you, I wouldn't fucking be here right now. I'd be dead, and you..." He trails off, shaking his head. "I don't even want to think about what they would've fucking done to you." He clenches his teeth, but his hold on my hand remains gentle. "Angel, what they did to you, it wasn't right. Nobody deserves that. My only regret is that I couldn't kill that bastard for you."

"You would've killed him for me?"

Without hesitation, he declares, "Fuck yes. Nobody, least of all you, deserves that kind of treatment."

I blink up at him, unsure how to process that. Why least of all me? Why me at all?

"I'm grateful to you, Angel. For calling Judge. For getting us both out. I could've accepted dying in there, because it would've meant I kept my club safe, but you? It would've haunted me in the afterlife."

His words settle into my heart, warming me from the inside out. No one has ever shown me the kindness Priest has in the short time I've known him. No one has ever made me feel worthy of anything, let alone their gratitude.

This man is my savior. I owe him everything, including my life.

Slipping off the bed, Priest's eyes go wide as I pull my shirt up and over my head.

"Boo, what the fuck are you doing?"

In answer, I drop to my knees and attempt to reach into his sweatpants, only to be stopped when he grabs my wrists.

"No, Boo," he snaps, his voice husky and deep. "As much as I love the sight of you before me, this isn't how I want you."

His rejection hits me like a punch to the gut. I've never willingly gone to my knees for any man, and the first time I do, he rejects me. Why am I not good enough? Does he see me as unclean? Damaged goods?

Priest had witnessed my degradation firsthand. The thought of that humiliation brings about my doubt and self-loathing. "I just wanted to thank you."

"I'm not that fucker, Angel. I don't need you to suck me off to thank me."

Releasing my wrists, he moves toward the door. My heart hammers against my chest as panic sets in. I've messed up. Priest doesn't want me. He's disgusted by me.

His hand is on the doorknob when he peers over his shoulder at me, still on my knees. "You deserve better than this. The life you knew in that clubhouse is gone, and in the past now. We take care of people here. We don't take sexual favors in return."

I just stare at him, not knowing what to say. My heart aches at the shame I'm feeling right now. "Are you leaving me?"

Priest's expression goes from defensive to intense as he meets my eyes. "No, Angel. I've got some business to tend to with the others, but I'll be back. I'm not leaving you. Not until you want me to."

With that, he steps out the door, leaving it open.

Open doors. No locks. His message is clear: this place isn't my prison. He's not my enemy. He may not want me, but he's not them. He's not my captor.

Chapter 19

PRIEST

"ALL RIGHT," Judge grunts, settling into his seat at the head of the table. "Looks like we're all here, so let's get started."

"Where's Hash?" GP asks, pointing toward his empty seat.

"Hashtag's working on a lead."

Judge doesn't elaborate on what that lead may be, but I can only hope Hash is on to wherever the Screwballs took off to when the club raided them the other day.

"How's the girl?" Judge asks, his gaze aimed at me.

I settle back in my seat. "Sore. Confused. Those fuckers have put her through hell, and it was going on long before they took me."

Judge nods, his jaw set in a hard line. "They'll get theirs. But we still don't know if we can trust her." He plucks a sheet of paper off the table and skims the writing. "Doc says she's on the mend. Her STD tests came back negative, and her wounds are healing."

I narrow my eyes, not liking the way he's talking about Boo, as if she's some sort of threat. She's not. She's a victim here.

"We need to talk to her, Priest," he advises, placing the paper back on the table. "We need to find out what she knows."

"Not now." This isn't the first time we've had this discussion, but this is the first time he's brought it up in church.

"It's not a request. I get the girl is roughed up, but we need answers if we're going to find these bastards. She may be the key to bringing them down."

I know he's right, but there's no way in hell Boo is ready for that kind of inquisition. "I said not now."

Judge studies me, his eyes hard and assessing. "You fuckin' her?"

His question hits me like a slap in the face. "No," I growl. "And if I were, it wouldn't be any of the club's business."

TK reaches over and places a hand on my shoulder. "Chill, man. Nobody's attacking you."

Standing from my chair, I shake him off, my body screaming in pain at the sudden movement, but I'm too pissed off to care. "They rape those women," I say to the men in the room, looking each one of them in the eye.

"They buy them, keep them in shitty conditions, barely feed them, and they fucking use them like their personal sex toys. One of them raped Boo right in front of me. I saw it in her eyes when he fucking broke her, and now you want to barge in there and ask her to tell you all about it? I don't fucking think so."

The silence in the room is so loud, you can hear a pin drop.

"Look, I know they're after the boy, TK, and if they come, I'll be leading the fucking charge to protect him, but he's not the only person we need to keep safe. Nobody's ever protected Boo, but she has me now, and I'm not letting anyone near her until I know she's ready."

Without hesitation, TK nods in understanding.

I turn to Judge, who doesn't look pissed anymore. He just looks frustrated. "I get it. I get what you're saying, and I feel for that girl. So, we can give it a bit more time, but we need to talk to her, and soon."

I take my seat, just as Hashtag bursts through door, announcing, "I got something!"

Hash is our tech guy, and he's damn good. Someone goes missing? He's the one to find them. If someone tries to break in? They need to get through his system first. And if we need intel on anything, Hash will fucking find it. Dude is a bloodhound for information.

"That girl," he says, his eyes meeting mine. "She's not who she says she is."

Jesus Christ. What is it with these guys attacking Boo?

Before I have a chance to argue, Hash moves toward Judge, hands him a stack of papers, and poses to the group, "Any of you ever heard of the Atlantic City Syndicate?"

"Aren't they the ones who took out that cartel outside of the casino?" StoneFace asks.

Hashtag's growing excited now. "That's the one. Fucking ruthless bunch. They're an Irish mafia group that runs the strip in Atlantic City."

"What does this have to do with Boo?" I huff, frustrated, just wanting to get back to my room.

"Well," he drawls. "Seems that Boo is the little sister of Liam Collins, the head of the whole fucking organization."

My eyes go wide.

Staring at the printouts in his hands, his eyes as wide as mine, Judge bellows, "You saying that girl in Priest's room is a fucking mafia princess?"

Hashtag smirks. "And Collins has been on a tear for years trying to find her."

I can't breathe. *A mafia princess?* There's no way she knows... or does she?

Chapter 20

BOO

WHILE PRIEST IS GONE, I take the time to get my hair sorted. The pink is fading more by the day, and the thought of it being completely gone makes me sad. My coppery red roots are already showing. I don't hate the red, but I like my pink better, because it feels more like me. I'd chosen to dye it, and it was one of very few decisions I'd ever made for myself.

Instead of plaiting it into a braid like I usually do, I let the length hang loose around my shoulders. The braids were always at Alan's insistence. *Better to hold you down with.* Now that I'm free of him, I doubt I'll ever braid it again.

I look over at the open door. I'm free to leave, free to roam, yet I can't, because I don't know what's out there. All I know is that I'm safe in this room, and leaving that scares me more than I want to admit, so I head back to the bed and make myself comfortable.

"Hey, Angel." Priest walks into the room with a sandwich and potato chips.

"I don't think I'm hungry enough to eat again. Not yet, at least," I say, though I accept the plate.

"Yes, you do. You're skin and bones."

I peer down at my body. I'd never been self-conscious, but suddenly, I feel inadequate, thanks to his earlier rejection. Is my body the problem? Am I too skinny? Are my breasts too small?

Priest drops his ass onto the bed in front of me. "What's that face?"

"Nothing," I mumble, my gaze falling to the plate on my lap. "I'm just not used to someone caring if I've eaten, or how skinny I am." As long as my pussy still worked and my legs opened, that's all that mattered to the Screwballs. "So, where'd you go?"

"Church."

I consider that. "It's about what to do with me, isn't it?"

"No, Angel." He grabs my hand and pulls it into his lap. "I briefed the guys on what happened with the Screwballs, that's all. Pretty routine, considering what happened."

"I can't stay here forever."

Part of me would like to stay right here, with him, for

the rest of eternity. But I know that once I've served my purpose, I'll be out on my ass and all alone.

He gives my hand a squeeze. "Why not?"

"I've been around clubs long enough to know how this works. Once I'm no longer useful, I'm gone."

"You can stay here as long as you want, and you don't have to do anything for anyone. You're here so we can keep you safe. Not because you have some sort of purpose."

I stare down at our entwined hand. "What if that changes?"

"It won't. The club has been working around the fucking clock to secure this place. Until this shit with the Screwballs is settled, we're working to protect everyone, and that includes you. You're not going back there or anywhere else you don't want to be. I'll make damn sure of it."

The fierceness in his tone surprises me, and I look up to meet his gaze. "You barely know me. Hell, I don't even know myself. I don't even know my last name. I've always been just Boo. I had an uncle once, but he sold me off to the Screwballs when I was just a kid. That's it. My entire life's story in a nutshell."

Priest's demeanor changes. "What if I told you that's not the end of your story?"

I frown. "What do you mean?"

Pulling his phone out of his pocket, he types in his

password, not bothering to hide it, and clicks on an icon, lighting up the screen with an image.

"Do you recognize any of these faces?" He hands me his phone. On the screen is an image of a family. I study their faces. The mother and father stand proudly in the center, with two kids flanking either side. A boy, about five, with light red hair, and a girl, who couldn't be older than three, with copper hair, all smiling at the camera.

"No," I say after a moment, handing the phone back to him. "Who are they?"

"They're your family, Boo."

I lean back, blinking in surprise. "I don't have any family besides my uncle."

Priest squeezes my hand and scoots closer. "I don't think that man was your uncle, Angel. We have reason to believe he's the one who took you from your family."

My gut twists and I reel back, shaking my head vigorously. No, that's not possible. I'd remember that, wouldn't I? I mean, my memory of my time with the Screwballs is fuzzy, but having an actual family—a mother and a father and a brother? I'd remember that.

Priest shifts, his face filled with compassion. "One of the guys, Hashtag, is this computer genius. He can find out anything if given the time. When they brought us in, Doc took a blood sample and your fingerprints. We still don't know for sure about the blood because someone Hash knows is still working on that, but your prints hit in a missing kids database. Your name isn't Boo, it's Bria. Bria Collins."

Bria Collins. The name carries a hint of familiarity that wraps around my heart. A family. A real one. I have a family. I have a name. After all this time… I'm not alone.

My heart races as I attempt to tamp down the excitement growing there. "Do you know where they are?"

"That's where it's a bit complicated. We think that when your "uncle" took you, your family was killed. Your grandfather was a mob boss, and there was hit. We're not sure by who, but the whole thing made national news. Their deaths, along with your picture, listed as a missing child."

Dead parents. Kidnapping. Mob boss. I shake my head. This story grows more ridiculous the more he reveals. It's like the plot for an action thriller movie. Stuff like this doesn't happen in real life.

The excitement that'd been building snuffs out like an unwelcome flame. "It's not true."

"I wouldn't believe it either if the roles were reversed, but we have every reason to believe it's true. Think about it. Why did the Screwballs keep you for so long? There had to be a reason."

He's right about that. The Screwballs rotated their women in and out like clockwork. Most only spent a few days before being shipped off to new owners. So, why had I been there for thirteen years? And why did Big Dick insist on keeping me alive?

"My uncle owed them money," I blurt out.

"I don't think that's true."

Blood rushes through my veins, pounding in my head as I consider this. Could this be why Big Dick kept me around?

Priest squeezes my hand again, snapping me back to reality. "Tell me what you're thinking, Angel."

"Big Dick," I whisper. "He told me he was about to get a big payday for me the night we got rescued."

Priest nods. "Your brother has been tearing the world apart looking for you. Hashtag reached out through his channels. He's coming here."

He's coming here? A brother I didn't know I had is coming here to take me away? The world slows around me and my head swims.

"Boo?" Priest calls, his words sounding hollow and too far away. "Breathe, sweetheart."

I can't breathe. *He doesn't want me to stay. I'm being taken away again.*

I start gasping for air as my vision grows dark around the edges.

Suddenly, Priest pulls me into his arms and crashes his lips to mine. The urgency in his kiss drags me back to reality, and I freeze, feeling so confused. As soon as he notices, he pulls away.

"Come back to me," he urges, his eyes searching mine. "Breathe, sweetheart. One right after another." He chants the words over and over again, until finally, my heart calms, and the oxygen flows to my lungs without issue. "Talk to me, Angel."

"You're sending me away," I respond, unable to look at him. "You don't want me to stay. You told me I could, but you're sending me away with this brother I don't even know."

He reaches up and grips my chin, his nose inches away. "I'm not sending you anywhere. We're just trying to find your family. Hell, he may not even show. He may never get our message, but we had to try. For you both." His dark eyes bore into my soul, like he's trying to figure out how to fix me. "Angel, the last thing I want is for you to leave me."

He's lying. "Why?" I bite out, frustrated with the rollercoaster of emotions I can't seem to escape. "You don't even want me. You pushed me away when I tried to thank you."

"Baby," he breathes, resting his forehead against mine. "I pushed you away because what you were doing was reflex. Those sons of bitches trained you to do that shit. You weren't doing it because you wanted to, but because of some twisted payment." He pulls back and lowers his face, forcing me to meet his gaze as he says, "Make no mistake, I sure as hell want you, Boo, but not like that. Never like that."

I hold his stare, baffled. He just said that he wants me. "Is that why you kissed me?"

"I kissed you because I needed to get your attention. Granted, it's not how I envisioned our first kiss, but I couldn't think of anything else to do. You were freaking out, and I had to get you back."

My fingers trace my lips, the memory of his lips still lingering there. My first kiss. My first *real* kiss. Not one stolen or forced upon me, but one freely given.

"Was that your first kiss?"

I nod, uncertainty nipping at my thoughts. "Thank you," I say, unable to look at him another second. "I've never been kissed like that before. I was a slave to them, a body to use. They never cared what any of it felt like for me."

"Kissing and touching should always be pleasurable, Angel. Especially if it's with someone who cares for you."

"Kiss me again. Touch me. Show me."

I watch as Priest's thoughts and my request war inside his mind, and just when I think he's going to reject me again, he reaches for me, wrapping his hand around the back of my neck, and pulls my lips to his.

"I'll show you how it should be," he whispers, his

lips brushing against mine as he speaks. "I'll show you a man's touch should never come with pain."

He doesn't move. His lips are touching mine, but we're still not kissing. He's waiting to see if this is what I truly want.

I do want it, even though the dark recesses of my mind are arguing against it. Sex isn't for pleasure, it's transactional. They fuck you, and then they leave. What if it's no different with him? I'm not sure my heart could take it.

But this is the first time I've had a choice. The first time a man has cared if I wanted his touch. And I've never wanted anyone's touch ever, until now.

"Kiss me," I breathe.

Chapter 21

PRIEST

FUCKING HELL. Boo's lips are soft and hesitant at first, but as I pull her closer, angling my head and deepening our kiss, she relaxes. My cock is already rock hard, but no matter what happens here, I won't push it. I won't fuck her. That's not what this is.

This is my chance to prove to this woman that a man's touch can be tender, and that her needs can be the sole focus. My cock will have to wait until I can take care of myself in the privacy of the shower.

Slowly, Boo's tongue presses against the seam of my mouth, and when I open for her, she slips it inside, caressing my tongue with hers, sending shivers along my spine. She's trembling now, but the way she presses on, I know it's from excitement and not from fear.

My head swims, threatening to carry me into oblivion,

but I force myself to stay put. I have to be present. I have to be aware of her every move, because one tiny hint of fear, and this ends. But for now, she's giving as much as I am.

Her hot breath mingling with mine, she lifts herself up and straddles my hips, angling her head down as she takes advantage of her new position, exploring my lips with hers, her fingers running through my hair.

"Touch me," she pleads.

Fucking hell.

Moving my hands from her hips, I run them up her sides, over the bulky T-shirt, then cup her breasts in my palms, my thumbs grazing her nipples through the material.

She gasps, her lips parted over mine, her eyes boring into me at the sensation.

"You like that, Angel?" I ask, barely recognizing my own fucking voice. It's deep and hoarse, and filled with need.

Pulling her lower lip between her teeth, she nods slowly as I do it again. Her nipples pebble beneath the pad of my thumb and her hips rock, her center brushing across my cock.

I give her time to process the sensation, and then she moves again, this time reaching for the hem of her shirt and pulling it up over her head. Her pink hair falls across her lightly freckled shoulders, the ends curling, brushing against her nipples, as if pointing to where I need to be focusing my attention.

The look in her eyes melts me. Fear. Pleasure. Need.

Gripping her waist, I keep my gaze on hers as I pull her higher, bringing her nipple to my lips. I press a soft kiss to one, and then the other, reveling in the way her cheeks flush. A tiny gasp escapes her lips as I flick my tongue out, dragging it over the tender bud.

My cock strains against my pants, yearning to connect with her, but it's not time.

Her breasts are perfection. Small and perky, tipped with strawberry nipples. I take my time, paying them homage, ignoring my own body's reaction as she moans and gasps on top of me.

She's wet, though. I can feel it. Her excitement has soaked through the thin material of her shorts and through my jogging pants.

"Take your shorts off."

She doesn't hesitate. Tilting to the side, she drags the shorts down, over her hips and off her legs, then tosses them to the side before settling back into place.

"You're so fucking beautiful," I whisper, pulling her lips to mine once more.

Her hips are rolling again, except now my pants are all that's keeping me from sliding deep inside of her.

I reach down, my fingers finding her wet center, the pad of my thumb rubbing against her clit.

She gasps, her body going still as I move my thumb in slow, gentle circles. "Priest."

"Does it feel good, Angel?"

She nods, but that's not enough for me. "Need the words, baby."

"Yes," she purrs. It feels so good."

Keeping the rhythm of my thumb going, I run my index finger farther down, then slowly sink it inside. Boo throws her head back, her hands gripping my shoulders as she lets out a long, low moan.

I rub her, fucking her pussy with my hand as she gasps, her cries of pleasure testing the limits of my restraint. She's close to coming. I can feel her body gripping my finger, and it's about to happen. But as much as I want her to, I need to taste this woman. I want her release on my tongue.

"Hold on, baby," I growl, rising from my position on the bed, ignoring my body's protests of pain as I flip her, laying her out on the mattress and towering above her.

She reaches for my cock, but I push her hand away. Reaching for her knee, I spread her legs open, her wide eyes watching as I lower myself between them.

Her pussy is glistening, and she smells like fucking heaven.

Her fingers tangle into my hair as I hold her gaze and flick my tongue through her folds. Her grip tightens when I kiss her swollen nub tenderly—once, twice, three times. Pulling my head closer, she rolls her hips.

"Please," she begs. "God, please."

BANG!

The door to my room bursts open. Burnt is standing there, his eyes wide and filled with fear as a man stands behind him, a gun pressed to the back of his head. Several men I don't know begin filing into the room.

"What the fuck?" I roar, clamoring up off the bed while shoving Boo's naked body behind me.

Then Judge, Hash, TK, and StoneFace rush in behind them, guns in their hands, but pointed down.

Two men I don't know approach the bed, but I don't have time to reach my gun. They're on me before I can blink, yanking me from the bed and away from Boo.

I fight back, my fists and legs flying. I manage to get in a couple of good hits before two other men move forward and grab me.

"Priest," Judge snaps. "Chill."

Easy for him to say. His room wasn't just invaded in the middle of an intimate fucking moment. He also has a gun in his hand, I don't.

"What the fuck is going on?" I seethe.

Boo is on the bed, the blankets pulled up under her chin, her terror filled gaze darting around the room.

"Put some fucking clothes on," the man with the gun aimed at Burnt snarls. Boo doesn't move, so he bends forward, grabs her discarded T-shirt, and tosses it at her. "Now!"

I struggle, desperate to get to her, to protect her from these men, but I don't even know who they are.

"Let's all just relax," Judge barks out, his hands going up, attempting to ease the tension. "This is a misunderstanding, so let's all just put our guns away and talk this through like men."

"A misunderstanding?" the man roars. "I come in here to find this big fucker with her naked in his bed, and that's some kind of misunderstanding?"

"Fuck you," I roar, struggling, wanting nothing more than to rip into him.

A fist lands in my gut and I double over, the air knocked from my lungs.

"Let's just talk this through," Judge tries again.

The man releases his hold on Burnt and moves toward the bed. I fight like hell to stop him, but I can't shake the four men holding me back. "I won't say it again. Put some fucking clothes on."

I expect her to show fear, but now she just looks angry. Grabbing the shirt, she slips it over her head and releases the blankets from around her. Once she's covered, she stands, her head barely coming to the strange man's shoulder. I can see she's about to lose it.

"Look, asshole. I don't know who you are, or who the hell you think you're talking to, but I'm sick and fucking tired of men thinking they can order me around like a dog. Either put the guns away or fucking shoot me, but I am over this macho bullshit."

The man's eyes grow wide, and then slowly, a smirk forms at the corner of his mouth. "Oh, yeah." Tucking the gun into the holster hooked to his belt, he backs away, stating, "You're definitely my sister."

Boo assesses him while crossing her arms over her chest. "Well if I'm your sister, you're not making a very good first impression."

BOO

FIERY ANGER COURSES through my veins, settling low in my belly. I'm tired of being a victim. I'm tired of just standing by and complying. Not this time. I don't care who he is. Never fucking again.

Priest struggles against his captors as the man who claims to be my brother tips his head back and laughs. "And you in a bed with a man's face between your legs is a good first impression?"

"Let him go," I order, nodding at Priest. "And put the guns away."

"Like hell," the man chuckles sarcastically. "These fuckers have been keeping you from me long enough, and they're going to be dealt with."

"Keeping me from you?" I challenge incredulously. "They just told me about you tonight. I didn't even know you existed. Hell, I don't even know your name."

Closing my eyes, I take a calming breath and open them again. "Now let him go, and put those guns away. They scare me, and there's no need for them."

The man's confused gaze stays trained on me, assessing my words. He then looks over at Judge. "How long have you had my sister?"

Judge lifts his hands high, showing the gun still in his hand, then makes a show of tucking it into the waistband of his pants. "Five days," he replies. "We just found out who you were today. Our buddy tried to get a message to you."

Nobody moves as he processes this information. After a moment, he looks back at me. "These men holding you hostage?"

I glare at him. "These men saved me. And I'm not answering any more of your questions until you put the guns away and let him go."

"We didn't take her," Priest growls, his face twisted in anger.

"Like I'd believe you, motherfucker," the man snaps.

"Then how about believing me?" I cry. "This man and his club saved me from some very bad men."

"I have proof they took you," he insists, but he doesn't sound so sure now.

Judge asks, "What proof?"

The man pulls a cell phone from the pocket of his

business suit, taps the screen a few times, and tosses it to me. "Look for yourself."

It's the image of a woman, bloody, beaten, and tied to a chair. My mouth drops and my gut twists. That poor woman. But there's one thing… the woman in the photo has red hair. Mine is pink.

"That's not me," I tell him. "My hair isn't red, and it hasn't been for a very long time."

The man steps forward and takes the phone from my hand, his brow furrowed as he studies it. His eyes go from the photo to me and back again.

Lowering my voice, I explain, "They tricked you," hoping maybe now, he'll finally understand.

"They could've forced you to dye it." His voice is defiant, but his expression remains puzzled.

Rolling my eyes, I twirl a lock around my fingers. "Look how faded it is. I've only been here a few days. This is a month's worth of fading. It was literally pink-pink."

"Then who is this?"

"Another girl…" Bile rises in my throat at the thought of her going through the torture they caused, just to perpetuate their lie. A lie that worked too. "The Screw-balls are fucking with you. They're using you to take out the Black Hoods."

He shakes his head, his brow furrowing as he struggles to understand. "Why would they do that?"

I'm done with this shit. "Put down the guns, let Priest go, and then we'll talk."

He quietly looks around the crowded room. "And if I don't?"

"You all end up killing each other for no reason at all."

I can see him struggling with everything he's been told, and then finally, he looks at one of his men and nods.

As one, his goons lower their weapons and release Priest. The Black Hoods follow suit, and Priest moves in my direction, but my "brother" jams a hand into his chest.

"No. Until I know what the fuck is going on here, you stay away from her."

"Like hell," Priest growls. "She's mine."

His words send an unpleasant jolt through my body. Since when did I become his? He said nobody owned me.

"She's my fucking sister. Don't think for one second that I'm going to ignore what I saw when I walked into this room."

Priest stands tall, towering over everybody in the room. "What you saw was none of your goddamn business."

God, this is so embarrassing. My face burns, and I'm willing to bet it's as red as my hair should be. "Stop," I say, wishing I could crawl into a hole and never come out. "Just let him by and leave the room. I'd like to get dressed so we can get this sorted."

His eyes narrow at me. "I'm not leaving you here with him."

"If you want to talk to me, I need to get dressed. And he's staying. This is his room, and he's the only person I trust right now."

Anger, confusion, and frustration flicker behind his green eyes. After a few moments, he seems to come to his senses and steps aside. "Fine. Five minutes. You have five minutes, and if you're not out of this room, I'm coming back for you."

With another nod, the men in the room head out, leaving me alone with Priest. As soon as the door closes, Priest moves, pulling me against his chest. "Jesus Christ, Angel. Are you okay?"

"I'm fine," I squeak out, my body trembling from the adrenaline rush. "That was terrifying. And also, if that really is my brother, I wish he hadn't walked in on what we were doing."

Priest chuckles, his chest vibrating against my cheek as he squeezes me a little tighter. "Trust me, I feel the same way. But I won't apologize. What we were sharing…" He shakes his head. "Fuck. You trusted me, and that means the fucking world to me. I just wish we hadn't been interrupted."

"You don't regret it?" I ask, hating how needy I sound.

"Never, Angel. This thing between us runs deeper than just a chance meeting while we were both captive. What we have is real, and I don't want it to end."

"I think so too," I admit, my voice quiet and unsure.

Leaning down, he parts my lips with his, sending my heart right back into overdrive.

A heavy knock at the door has us both jumping. "Three minutes," a voice calls out, reminding us that our moment will have to wait.

Priest pulls away, but stares down at me, his face filled with fire. "I promise you, Boo, that so long as I'm breathing, nobody will harm a single hair on your head. From now on, it's me and you against the fucking world."

I smile, unsure of how to respond, but my heart flutters. He really does want me. He wants us.

"Let's get you a change of clothes. I think we're down to two minutes."

Priest retrieves my shorts and panties from the floor. Thankfully, his shirt had been long enough to hide myself from the audience that had joined us, but it did nothing to lessen the embarrassment. He kneels down on the floor and holds my panties out so I can step into them, then does the same with my shorts. The memory of his face between my legs plays in my mind as he slips the garments up my legs and over my hips, his face just inches away from where he'd been not so long ago.

He must be remembering too, because he peers up at me from the floor, a sexy smile on his lips. "The next time I'm between your legs, there'll be no interruptions."

Butterflies swarm in my belly as I stare down at him, all thoughts of the seriousness of our current situation the farthest thing from my mind.

"Are you ready for this?" Rising from the floor, he pulls me against his chest once more. "If you don't want to talk to him, you don't have to."

"No." I sigh. "I need to know. I need to know the truth, and so does he."

Priest nods and presses a kiss to the top of my head. "I'm with you every step of the way, sweetheart. You and me against the world."

PRIEST

WHEN WE STEP out into the main room, we step into what feels like an oncoming war. The Black Hoods stand on one side, their hands ready to draw their weapons at any second. The other group of men stand across from them, their eyes narrowed, taking in the scene.

As soon as they see us, the ringleader moves, coming for Boo much faster than I'm comfortable with.

Holding up a hand, I push her behind me and the man stops. "Stay back," I warn him. "She's not ready for an ambush. You can talk, but you do it sitting on opposite sides of the table, and you do it with me present."

He doesn't like it, but one look at Boo and he knows it's the right move. With a brisk nod of his head, he asks, "Where can we be alone?"

"The table," Judge says, stepping forward. "Where

we hold our meetings. You can sit in there, but you leave the door open. Now that we know how you got past our security, you won't take us by surprise a second time."

"It pays to have one of the best hackers out there." Smirking, he heads in the direction Judge is pointing to.

Boo's tiny hand slips into mine, and I give it a gentle squeeze as we follow him. Her trust in me is not something I take lightly. She makes me feel bulletproof. And for her, I will be.

The man takes a seat at the head of the table, the place reserved for the club's president. It's a power move. His way of saying that he's the one in charge here. Boo takes a seat at the opposite end, as far away from him as she can, never once releasing her grip on my hand.

"Who sent me that picture?" he starts.

"What's your name?" Boo asks in return, ignoring his question.

This seems to catch him off guard. Frowning, he tells her, "Liam. Liam Collins. And you're my sister, Bria."

Silence hangs in the air as Boo considers that. "Bria Collins," she says, testing the name for the first time.

"You were taken away when you were just five years old," he goes on, the authority gone from his tone. "Do you have no memory of me or our family?"

Boo shakes her head, her lips pursed together.

Neither one of them speak for a long time, they just

stare at each other. They look so much alike. Even the way Liam's head tips to the side when he's thinking is something I've seen Boo do a million times already.

Liam gets to his feet and walks toward the end of the table. I stay on alert as he hesitantly takes a seat next to Boo. "Who took you?" he questions. "I've been looking everywhere for you."

"I don't know," she whispers. "All I know is that my uncle gave me to the Screwballs MC when I was just ten years old, and I don't have a lot of memories before that. I had lived with my uncle for a couple of years before that, but anytime I try to remember my life before him, things get all jumbled up. He used to tell me lies and stories, and he confused me on what had been real and what he had told me was real."

"The Screwballs," Liam mutters, his gaze darting to me. "And who are the Screwballs?"

"Very fucking bad men," I growl. "Their president goes by the name of Big Dick, and he's as fucked-up as they come. He has a whole club full of men who think nothing of raping and trafficking women."

Liam's jaw ticks as he absorbs that information. "And how did you come into the picture?"

"Big Dick's boy is with us. The boy's mother is with one of our men, and he wanted his boy back. Forced me to wreck my bike and took me hostage."

Liam nods and leans back in his chair, crossing his

ankle over his knee as he turns his attention back to Boo. "This true?"

She nods. "I saw them bring him in. I managed to talk to him a couple of times, and he asked me to call Judge. They rescued us both a few days later."

"Why did they send me that picture?"

A tear slips from Boo's eye and rolls down her cheek. "I don't know."

"Who is the woman in that picture?"

Another tear falls. "I don't know."

"Why would they tell me you took my sister?" he asks me.

"I was their favorite slave," Boo interjects, her voice filled with sadness. "One man, Alan, he considered me his personal property. He would never let me go without a fight." She squeezes my hand and continues. "It's obvious they wanted you to charge in here and kill them yourself so they wouldn't have to. Their hands would seem clean, and they could still get the money they wanted for me."

The impact of her words washes over him. He goes to reach for her hand, pausing midair before he stops. "What did they do to you, Bria?"

"It wasn't just me," she says softly. "There were a lot of women. They bought and sold us, and use us while they had us. We cooked and cleaned, and whenever they wanted…" She takes a shaky breath. "They used us for whatever they wanted, whenever they wanted, and we were forced to give it to them."

I don't know if it's redheads in general, or just Irish people, but Liam has the same telling blush I've seen on Boo many times, though his isn't a blush of embarrassment. It's a flush of rage.

"They raped you?"

Boo nods.

"They beat you?"

Boo nods again. Her confirmation hits me like a bullet. I knew how bad it was, but the idea that this had been going on since she was just a child fucks with my self-control.

"And what was the name of this uncle who sold you to them?"

"I only ever knew him as Uncle."

Liam leans forward, his eyes leveling with Boo's. "That man was not your uncle. And if he's still alive, I'll kill him myself."

I want to argue with that. After everything Boo and I have been through together, I want to be the one to take that sick fuck out for her. But from the look on his face, I can see that he didn't just do that shit to her. He may not have sold Liam the way he did Boo, but he wronged their family in a way I still don't understand. He destroyed them. His blood needs to be on Liam's hands.

His chair scrapes across the floor as he jumps to his

feet and paces the room, his anger coming off of him in waves. "He's a dead man. They're all dead men."

"That's the plan," I say, placing a hand on Boo's trembling shoulder.

Liam pauses. "We need a new plan, and we need it now." He moves to the door and looks out at the men in the main room. I watch as he motions to someone, and a few moments later, Judge steps into the room.

"Everything settled now?"

Liam nods, the movement dismissive, his wheels already spinning on his next move. "What's the plan?" he asks, his gaze leveling with Judge's.

Judge grins. "I thought you'd never ask."

BOO

LORD, they've been in that room for a long time. I can't keep from staring at the door separating me from Priest and my brother. There's been no shouting or fighting, so it must be going well. After they'd let me tell my story, Judge had asked me to step outside. Priest had tried to come with me, but Judge ordered him to stay, my usefulness to the current discussion clearly over.

"If you keep staring at the door, you'll go crazy," a voice remarks, breaking into my thoughts. A woman with red hair joins me on the couch, cradling a baby in her arms. "Trust me, once they go in there to solve the problems of the world, it can take days."

I say nothing as I stare back at her. Women have never been kind to me. Hell, most of the women I've met over the years were captives, just like me. They would stab you in the back in an instant if it meant they could survive another day.

"Blair," the woman says, extending her hand. "I'm GP's ol' lady, and this is our daughter, Henley." She shifts the sleeping infant in her arms. Under her little black Harley hat is a swatch of red hair, like her mother's.

Tentatively, I take her hand in mine and give it a quick shake. "How old is she?"

Blair smiles. "Six weeks." The little girl stirs, snuggling in tighter.

"They're cute when they're that age," another woman says, joining us. She has a short pink and blonde bob haircut, and her skin is covered in tattoos. Two other women approach, hot on her heels. "Just wait until they become teenagers and hormones hit. The hormone monster lives at my house permanently. My sweet little Hayden is gone. Now it's all grunts and being glued to her phone."

"Shelby," she says with a soft smile, then points at the others. "This is Cora, and this is Grace." Each woman wave as they settle into the loveseat across from us. "Lindsey and Delilah wanted to be here, but they couldn't get away from work."

Work? They're allowed to work?

"I know you probably have a lot of questions," Cora acknowledges, "but I need to thank you for what you did. You brought Priest back to us, and you protected my son."

Her son. Big Dick's son. The kid he's determined to take from his mother.

"I didn't do anything," I tell her, unsure of how to respond to any of this. All these women surrounding me is making me nervous.

"You did, honey," Grace adds. "You saved him, and Cora and Harrison in the process. He wouldn't be here without you."

"Oh no," I say, shaking my head. "Priest is the one who saved me."

"That's not the way we heard it, and trust me, sugar, pillow talk with these guys is all club business these days." Shelby smiles. "It's a nice break from Wyatt's rambling about some new computer chip coming out. The man could talk to a wall if it's about computers."

Wyatt. I don't recognize the name, but Priest had mentioned a member who likes computers. "Is he... Hashtag?"

"The one and only. But he's Wyatt to me."

"And you?" I ask the older woman of the group. "Are you with one of the guys too?"

"Judge," she replies, beaming. "That cantankerous bastard is all mine." The ladies erupt into laughter, as if there's an inside story that I'm missing, but I don't even care. I'm still trying to wrap my head around the fact that these women, all with lives of their own, are in actual relationships with the men of this club. It's all so foreign to me.

"Sorry," Grace says with a sheepish smile. "Once you get to know the guys, you'll understand the laughter. Life with them is interesting, to say the least."

I press my lips together in a failed attempt at a smile. "I wouldn't know about that."

"You will, honey. Give it time. We know you've been through a lot, which is why we haven't come barging in and meddling like we tend to do. I know things must feel upside down right now."

"That's an understatement." I snort. "One second, I'm a slave for the Screwballs, and the next, I'm here with Priest. Oh, and I have a brother I didn't know about, so basically, my life is like a soap opera."

Grace nods, placing a hand on my knee. "It's a lot to take in."

"But these men are good men," Blair boasts. "They may look like scary beasts, but they'll knock themselves out trying to help you."

A tear escapes my eye, quickly followed by another one. "It's all just so much," I admit.

"Of course it is," Grace says softly. "And you take all the time in the world to wrap your pretty little head around it. Judging by the way Priest looks at you, I don't think he wants you going anywhere anytime soon."

My face flushes as I think about what had been going on in Priest's room earlier.

"I see those feelings might be mutual," Blair chirps. "It's about time Priest found someone."

"About time?"

Blair nods. "Priest has always been different from the others. He doesn't chase women. Hell, I wondered if he even liked them."

I gape back at her, unable to hide my surprise. "You did?"

"Yep. But I suspect he was waiting for someone like you."

The heavy wooden door to the meeting room swings open then, and men wearing suits file out, followed by members of the Black Hoods. Several of the guys join their women in the sitting area. The love shared between these couples is apparent to everyone, even me. There's love here. Safety. Children.

A pang of guilt punches me in the gut. I would have missed out on all of this had stayed holed up in Priest's room. I guess I can thank my brother for forcing me out of the safety of the room.

Liam emerges, a scowl plastered on his face. Priest is hot on his heels, but passes him as he stalks toward me.

"We need to talk," Liam says, his eyes on me. "Now."

Priest turns, putting himself between us yet again. "You need to ask her if she even wants to talk to you, asshole. If she doesn't, you respect her fucking decision."

"It's okay," I tell them both, rising from the couch.

"You're sure?" Priest asks, reaching for my hand and giving it a gentle squeeze. "Want me to join you?"

I do. God, I do. But I need to handle this on my own. "No, it's better if I talk to him alone."

Priest analyzes my statement, clearly unhappy with my decision, but he doesn't argue. He just nods in agreement. "You can use the meeting room. It's clear now."

Without a word, Liam whips around and heads back to the meeting room, slipping through the open door.

You can do this, Boo... Bria...

Dread washes over me as I stare at the door. I have to do this. Not only for me, but for him. He lost a sister, and I lost everything. He deserves the truth of what happened as much as I deserve the truth of what happened to our family.

"The offer still stands," Priest reminds me, his body a warm presence at my side.

I sigh, dragging in a lungful of oxygen and courage. "No, I need to do this on my own."

Taking my hand, he leads me to the open door, stopping just short of stepping inside himself. "I'll be right out here."

He ushers me into the room and steps out, closing the door as he goes. It clicks as the latch catches, and I jump a little at the sudden noise. Liam sits in one of the empty chairs, his hands splayed across the large meeting table in the middle of the room. He doesn't look up when I enter.

"You wanted to talk," I say softly. "So here I am, Mr. Collins."

"Liam. You can call me by my given name." He doesn't move a single inch. His gaze never shifts from the hard, wooden table in front of him. "I need to know," his deep voice growls, the words cut off with a quivering gulp. "How long?" His tone is even sharper now. Sharp enough to cut the glass on the windows behind him. "How long did it go on?"

I move toward him then, still wary, but hating the pain I hear in his voice. "The day I turned eighteen. Or, at least, when they told me I turned eighteen. To be honest, I don't even know when my birthday is."

Liam groans, his fist slamming against the table. He recoils the second after the strike hits, cradling his hand against his chest.

I cry out, more from surprise than from fear. "Liam, your hand." I move closer to him, but he pulls away from me, shaking his head, and still not meeting my eyes. Is what happened to me so disgusting that even my own brother won't let me comfort him?

"I'm going to kill them for what they did to you, every last fucking one of them. That club is going to burn in hell for all of this." Red hot anger has the veins in his neck popping out farther with each passing second, the tattoos there doing nothing to hide them. "For taking you away from our family."

"So, you're going after them," I surmise. "You and the club?"

"Fucking right we are."

I don't know how to feel about his answer. Part of me wants them to do it, but what if they get hurt? What if I lose my brother before I even get a chance to know him? What if I lose Priest?

"When?"

"Not soon enough," he grunts.

Silence settles between us. Finally, his green eyes meet mine, sadness and anger swirling inside of them like a tempest about to collide with a ship at sea. "You look like her, you know?

Our mother."

Mother. I had a mother. Why can't I remember her? "Tell me about them, about our life before all this happened."

"You truly don't remember anything?"

I shake my head, ashamed at my own memory. "Nothing. I don't remember anything before all of this."

Liam stands and pulls out one of the chairs for me. I take the seat and he joins me, sitting in the chair next to mine.

"I don't even know where to start, Bria." I flinch at the name, but my brother is observant. He notices immediately. "Sorry," he says. "You'll always be Bria to me. I'm not sure I can call you Boo."

"You can call me that if it helps." I give him a tender smile. "Can you tell me about them?"

He leans back in his chair, his hands folded in his lap. "How do I summarize your life?"

I shrug. "The beginning might be best."

Liam's sigh carries the weight of the world on it as he begins. "Our grandfather was Declan Collins. He immigrated from Ireland when he was young, and met our grandmother, Una, at Ellis Island. They married young, settled in Atlantic City, and started their family. Our father, Cormac, came shortly after."

Cormac. It doesn't trigger any recognition.

"And our mother?"

"Saoirse." Again, the name triggers no memories. "Da always called her by her nickname, Sersh. He was already working for our grandfather when he met Mum, but he met her at a pub while visiting Ireland, and said it was love at first sight."

"Where did he work?"

It's odd, in a way, but I've never given much thought to who my parents were, or how I'd ended up with my uncle. The idea of a different life had always been too painful, but now that I'm learning about them, I just want to know every tiny detail.

"Casinos, mostly." Liam's lips twist to one side. "Among other things." When his eyes meet mine, he almost looks apologetic. "Our family has operated the Irish syndicate in Atlantic City for decades now. First grandfather, and now me."

I blink, my brain working double time to absorb that bombshell. Liam is a mob boss. That's why Priest had asked me about the mafia earlier. If my brother is a Don, what does that make me? Mafia royalty?

"Da was killed before he could take over, so now, it's all on me."

I swallow, my throat feeling tight and thick. "How did they die?"

Liam picks at some imaginary lint on his designer suit. "Grandfather made a bad deal and couldn't pay the debt. He was moving us to a safe house when they came. They took you first, grabbing you right out of your private Catholic school classroom. I was next. They pulled me right off the street. I'd skipped school that day. They got our parents when they went looking for you."

These new revelations tangle in my mind like fishing wire. "How do I not remember any of this? I want to believe you, but I can't recall a damn thing. How do I not remember being abducted from school."

Liam frowns, clearly just as confused as me. "I don't

know, Bria. The last time I saw you, you were unharmed."

"When was that?"

"The day our parents died." He pauses then, his eyes studying my face. "Are you sure you want to know this shit? Maybe not remembering how it happened is a blessing. All of it still haunts me, even now."

I consider his question. Would it be better to spare myself the pain, or would I rather know? I roll the decision around in my mind before I settle on the answer.

"I want to know."

Liam nods, clearly willing to let me make this choice. "The men who took us belonged to an old family. One our grandfather had been at odds with for years. He'd run into some money trouble after one of his casino's failed, and he borrowed more from the one family that had it to spare, the Kelly's. They held us all for ransom, demanding Grandfather pay them the money, plus a little extra to get us back. He didn't have it, of course. The new casino he'd built had only been open for a few weeks at that point, but they knew that. They'd planned it that way. When he didn't pay up, they shot Mum and Da in the head right in front of him, and us. When they turned the gun on you, grandfather pleaded for a trade —us for him."

"Did they take it?"

"They shot him where he stood."

God, so much violence. "What happened to us?"

"We were separated. I was sent to another one of their families, raised by them as the next Kelly foot soldier. You were just gone. No one knew where you went, Bebe."

The name pings something in my brain. "Say that again. What did you just call me?"

"Bebe."

"I've heard that name before." My mind swirls, memories flickering and blinking in and out of existence until one of a young boy with shaggy red hair stands before me, his hand outstretched. He tries to say something, but no sound comes out. "Did you call me that when we were little?"

Liam smiles for the first time. "I gave you that nickname the day you were born. I was the only one who called you that."

"I think I remember that. It's still foggy in here." I tap my head. "But there's something familiar about that name."

"It doesn't seem fair what you've been through. I was given the world when I came into our family's inheritance. I used that to put an end to the Kelly's and seized their assets, the same way I'm going to end that fucking club."

"What happens after that? What happens after it's done?"

"We go home, Bebe, where you belong. Where you've always belonged. Home with me, safe from all this shit."

Home. The word settles in my chest like a hug from an old friend. I'd dreamed of a home for so long, and now it's dangling in front of me like a carrot, just out of my reach. If I go home with Liam, I'd be leaving Priest behind. I'm not sure I can do that.

How do you just leave the person who makes you feel complete?

Chapter 25

PRIEST

I CLOSE the door to my room and pull her to my chest, wrapping my arms around her and squeezing her tightly. The pressure hurts like hell, but I don't care. This has been quite a day for both of us, and I'm so glad to finally have her alone so we can both decompress.

"You okay?" she asks, her voice muffled by my shirt against her lips.

Chuckling, I release her just a little, and place a kiss to the top of her head. "Good now."

She grins and pops up on her toes, pressing her mouth to mine. I return her kiss, but allow her to control it. This is the first time she's ever kissed me on her own. The first time she's initiated any affection toward me.

After a moment, she pulls away, smiles, and flops back onto the bed. "God, I'm so tired." Groaning, she rolls onto her side and props her head on her hand. "It's exhausting finding out you're a kidnapped mafia princess with a pissed off big brother and a string of Casinos."

Sitting down beside her, I rest my hand on her hip. "I'm afraid I have a bit more news, Angel."

"And what could that be?"

"We're moving in on the Screwballs tonight."

She bolts upright, her eyes wide with fear. "Tonight? So soon?"

I nod, wishing I could give her any other answer but this one. "We have to. The Screwballs have other women there, and we need to get them out. And I don't know if I can sleep another night knowing any of those sick fucks are still breathing air."

She swallows, tears springing to her eyes. "But you're hurt."

"I am, but I'm getting better, and there's no way in hell I'm sitting this one out. That bastard Alan has a bullet in my gun with his name on it."

Rising to her feet, I watch as she paces the floor, wringing her hands as she absorbs the news. "I can't lose you. I just found you… I just found me!"

Getting off the bed, I stop her pacing by resting my hands on her shoulders. "You're not gonna lose me, Bria."

The worry on her face melts away, replaced with a

look so soft, my heart skips a beat. "What did you call me?"

Shit. Maybe that was the wrong thing to say. "Bria. Your name isn't Boo, Angel. It never was. Those sick fucks called you that. I'll call you whatever name you want, but I won't call you Boo."

Her eyes search mine, and just when I think I've made the wrong call, she drops to her knees in front of me.

"Angel, no." I reach for her, but she pushes my hands away, reaching for the tie on my sweatpants. "You don't ever have to get on your knees for me."

When her gaze meets mine, it's filled with heat, and something that looks very similar to love. "I want to. I want to be with you," she says. "I want to taste you. I want you to finish what we started earlier, and I want to know what you feel like when you're inside of me."

Her words are determined, and they knock the breath from my lungs. I don't dare move a muscle as she reaches forward and pulls my cock out. She holds it in her hand, pausing as she looks at it, then her eyes lift to mine as she draws her tongue slowly up my length.

"Fuck," I groan.

My hands itch to bury themselves into her hair, to guide her head as she licks me, but I don't. Instead, I ball them into fists at my side and watch, not wanting to miss a single moment of her mouth on me.

Bria's eyes never waver from mine as she kisses my cock, running her hand slowly up and down. I didn't know it was possible to get so hard so fast, but clearly, it is.

She parts her lips and takes me into her mouth, swirling her tongue around and over as she moves her head up and down. Electric shocks shoot through my legs, sending fireworks through my body and settling low in my spine.

Placing my hand on her cheek, I tell her, "You keep doing that, baby, I won't make it to the part where I get inside of you."

Releasing my cock from her mouth, she grins up at me.

I reach for her hand and help her to her feet, pulling her against me as I claim her mouth. Her fingertips slide into my hair, clinging to me and holding me tighter, a soft moan escaping her and settling into my balls.

I haven't had sex in a very long time, and I've never had sex with someone who looks at me the way Bria does.

I take a step toward the bed and reach for her shorts. Dropping to my knees, I kiss her belly as I slide them down over her hips and down her legs. Once they're off, I press a kiss just above her folds, and in a husky voice, I whisper, "Lay on your back, Angel."

She does, without hesitation, and opens her legs for

me, her eyes on mine. I don't look away as I slide my tongue through her center, then flicking her clit. There's something about the way our eyes lock. Something growing.

Trust? Confidence? Love?

Whatever it is, it's strong, and everything shifts between us. This isn't just sex. This is a joining of souls and hearts. Of us.

Her release comes quickly, catching her off guard. I lap at her, swirling my tongue in tender circles as her eyes grow wide and her hips rock against my face. "God, Priest, yes. Right there. Don't stop... Please, don't fucking stop."

I'm not fucking stopping. I'm not even close to being finished with her.

Her body trembles before me, and a pink flush spreads across her cheeks as she moans my name.

"Baby," I croak out when her body stills. "I would love to do this all fucking night, but I need to feel you."

Digging her heels into the mattress, she scoots back onto it. "I need you too."

Popping to my feet, I rummage around in my night-stand and pull out a condom. Once I roll it down, I crawl over her and settle between her legs.

"You sure?" I ask her, praying she says yes, because if she isn't sure, I might explode.

She reaches for me, positioning my cock at her

entrance, and rolls her hips until the tip is just inside. "Fuck me, baby."

That's all I need to hear.

In one swift move, I enter her, burying myself deep inside. My eyes roll back as her slick walls hug me tightly. "Fuck," I hiss as Bria groans, "Oh, God."

I have to force myself to move slowly. I want to fuck her. I want to drive myself into her until we become one fucking person, but this is not the time. This time is about more than just getting off.

I move slowly, rolling my hips, reveling in the way she accepts me into her body.

"Priest," she coos, her hands coming up and resting on my cheeks.

"Mmm?"

"This feels good, baby. So very good. But I need you to fuck me now."

"Thank God," I mutter.

I pull away, my cock nearly crying at her sudden absence. Then I flip her onto her stomach and pull her up until she's on all fours. Her pussy glistens, ready and waiting for me, but it's her eyes I can't look away from. She's looking back at me, her eyes filled with greedy fire as I position myself behind her.

"You ready?"

She sinks her teeth into her bottom lip and nods.

Slamming inside of Bria is like coming home. Our

bodies fit together perfectly, our breathing matched and heavy.

I hold her gaze as I fuck her. It's the most erotic moment of my life, because I may be fucking her hard, but this is not just fucking. This is our union.

"Oh, God," she whimpers. "Oh, fuck. I'm gonna—"

And she does. Her pussy clamps down around me like a vice, quivering and squeezing. My own release hits me like a rocket, and my body trembles as my hips stutter, trying to keep a steady rhythm while my soul leaves my body.

Once our bodies still, I drop down beside her, my hand resting at the base of her spine. She turns to look at me, her head resting on her hands. "Can I tell you something?"

"Anything," I say, still trying to catch my breath.

Her smile is wide. "You were right. Sex isn't so bad after all."

BRIA

WATCHING them leave is probably the hardest thing I've ever had to do. The Black Hoods, along with Liam and the rest of his crew, are on a mission that could be the end of all of them. None of them know what's going to happen tonight. All they know is that the Screwballs are back at the clubhouse, conducting business as usual.

"Knock-knock," a voice calls from the door. A woman with light hair piled up in a messy bun leans against the doorframe. I notice the shirt she's wearing is identical to one of Priest's... the one I'm currently wearing. "Nice shirt. About time the bastard finally started using them. Or, well, you."

Pulling the material away from my body, I peer down at it. A pang of jealousy punches me in my already churning gut. Why would she have a shirt to match Priest's?

"I buy him one every year for Christmas," she explains, stepping into the room and extending her hand to me. "I'm Lindsey. Judge is my uncle, and Karma's my husband."

Relief washes over me. Meeting someone from Priest's past right now would've sent me into a tailspin.

"We made dinner if you'd like to join us. Having company certainly helps while the guys are on a run."

"Sure." Moving off the bed, I follow her out and toward the aroma of food coming from the kitchen. The smells are divine, smoky and sweet.

Lindsey ushers me to a table where several of the other ladies sit, a spread of food laid out in front of them. The men left behind to guard us are nowhere to be seen.

A group of teenagers sit around the big screen television with plates of food in their laps.

"Kids!" Grace calls to them. "Say hello to Bria."

The teens all turn their heads slowly, murmuring hellos before returning their attention back to the big screen.

"Sorry about them," she says, her lips twisting to one side. "Teenagers. Can't live with them at this age, I swear. Hungry?"

I stare at her. I haven't been invited to sit at a table for a full meal for as long as I can remember. "Famished," I tell her, spying an open spot at the end of the table. Before I can get it, Grace tugs me down next to her.

I settle into the spot, and my eyes go wide as I take in the amount of food in front of me. There's a huge platter of heavily sauced barbecue chicken, cornbread, and baked macaroni and cheese, with a thick layer of cheese cooked to a golden brown, flanked by even more delicious looking side dishes. My mouth waters as the aroma whirls around the table. How can anyone eat with so much going on? My stomach rumbles, telling me it might not be so hard after all.

"Eat up," Blair sings, placing a couple pitchers of beer down on the table.

As everyone digs in, I take scoops of everything, but the second the barbecue hits my lips, I know I'll be going back for seconds. I eat quickly, solely focused on the incredible food, and it's not until I reach for a second helping of chicken that I realize they're all staring at me, their mouths agape.

"Sorry," I mutter, wiping sauce from my chin.

"It's okay," Lindsey giggles, a grin taking over her face. "Stress eating. Trust me, we get it."

The ladies chatter amongst themselves as I finish my second helping. I consider a third, but stop when I notice Burnt walking through the back door. Everyone stops what they're doing, and turn to look at him.

"Nothing yet," he advises.

Grace nods. "No news is good news, right?"

"It's definitely not bad. Spare a plate for V and I?"

"Sure." Grace heads into the kitchen and returns a few minutes later with a stack of plates in her hands. "Liam's guys hungry too?"

"They'd have to talk to me to know that," he mutters.

"Did they hurt you?" I blurt out without thinking. I'd wondered about that since everything went down in Priest's room, but I'd been too worried about everything else to ask. "My brother, I mean."

"Nah, sugar. Takes more than a gun to the back of the head to rattle these nerves." He smacks his chest with his closed fist. "Wasn't the first time it's happened, won't be the last."

He had a gun to his head. How can he downplay that?

My question must show on my face, because Burnt shakes his head. "Sorry. Humor is how we deal with the hard shit, ya know?"

I didn't. Finding humor in the dark recesses of my life experiences is not something that's ever come easy to me. Those moments, like dark voids, ink their way into the few good moments I've had.

"Here you go," Grace says, passing the heaping plates to Burnt.

"Thanks for the grub, ladies. Back to work for me." He pivots on his heels and heads back out the door.

"Everyone processes things differently," Blair

confides. "Some like Burnt use humor to hide their trauma. Others find another outlet, like working out, or a hobby to distract themselves." I gaze over at Blair. Her soft, sweet smile is comforting.

"How do you all deal with this stuff? Does it happen all the time?"

"Not as much as you think. But lately, yeah, it's been bad. The club has been, how do I describe it…?"

"Busy," Grace interjects. "It's club life, Bria. The guys here do what others can't—protect the innocent. Is it always legal? No, but it gets the job done. With the way the world has been these last few years, it's gotten worse."

"How do you cope with it? With them being gone?"

"We do our best. We stick together for us, for the kids, and for them. They can go off into the wild blue yonder to take care of business because they know we'll hold down the fort at home." Blair's voice is even, and confident. She's speaking from experience, it appears. Though, seeing that sleeping baby in her arms, and knowing her husband is out there, going into a dangerous situation with an unknown outcome, terrifies me. This thing between Priest and I is so new. I can't imagine it would get easier with time.

"We have to be strong for them," Shelby adds. "This club found my daughter and brought her home safe."

"They saved me from a stalker," Blair reveals.

"They gave me a family," Grace declares.

Cora leans in close to me. "When I first got here, Blair and Lindsey were godsends for me and my son. I spent so much of my life living in fear of his father, I wasn't really living. TK gave me a safety net. One that can protect us all while we heal. That includes you, you know."

Blair reaches over and grabs Cora's hand, giving it a squeeze.

"They're our home. Sure, they have their faults. Temperamental moody bastards most of the time." The ladies laugh at that. "But they're ours, and we're theirs. It all works because we're strong for each other. We can be that for you too, if you'd let us."

Tears threaten to take over, and I swallow, fighting to hold them back. "I don't know where I fit into all of this," I admit. "There's so much I don't understand."

Blair nods. "And that's totally okay. The trauma you've been subjected to isn't just going to go away. It takes time, and finding someone you trust enough to help you work through it isn't easy, but I think you've found that in Priest."

I think about that for a moment and smile. She's right. Priest has become my rock. My safe place. He's given me things I never thought possible. Finding pleasure in life. Safety. Dare I say a family? One that won't use and abuse me?

"I know that smile," Grace says. "Seen it on every woman sitting here at this table. Have you told him how you feel?"

"It seems too soon."

"Nothing is too soon with these guys. Once they set their sights on you, they become cavemen and lay claim to you. Trust me, sugar, he knows, but he's waiting for you to tell him yourself."

Is it possible to fall this fast? To fall in love with a man who's seen my dark past firsthand and can look past it? My heart says yes, but my mind throws roadblocks at every turn. Tiny hesitations that leave me second-guessing. Once all of this is done with the Screwballs, would he still want me around? Would he still want me if I decide to join Liam back in Atlantic City?

There are too many questions and too few answers. The answers will have to wait, though. First, I need him to come back to me safe and sound.

If he comes back at all...

If he doesn't, I'll be shattered, because I think I love him.

I think I love Priest.

PRIEST

AS MUCH AS I'd tried to convince Bria that I was well enough to drive, I'd clearly been lying to both of us. The drive to the Screwballs clubhouse had taken hours, and even though Judge refused to let me take my bike, just sitting in the van for so long has been torture.

We pull up together, parking along a side street void of any streetlights, and in full view of the Screwballs pathetic looking compound. The walk to the gates takes longer than I'd anticipated, and my broken ribs are screaming.

Two men stand on either side of the tall metal gate. Even though I can't see their guns, I know damn well they're packing. The Screwballs are expecting us, and they won't leave any room for surprises.

Liam kneels down low between Judge and me. "Now what?"

Judge's brow is pulled low over his eyes as he assesses the scene before us. "We need to create a distraction. Pull their attention away while the others slip inside."

"Fuck that," StoneFace growls, his rifle raised and pointed at the gate.

"StoneFace," Judge barks quietly, careful not tip off the Screwball's guards. "StoneFace, get back here."

StoneFace ignores Judge's orders and tells me, "I'll have these gates cleared in just a minute. You fuckers be ready to move in."

Judge curses, throwing his hands in the air before turning to signal to the others to get ready.

I watch in silence as StoneFace strolls into the circle of light in front of the gate. "Hey, assholes!" he shouts.

The two men whip around, one of them with a cigarette dangling from between his lips. They don't even get a chance to say a word before StoneFace puts a bullet between their eyes, one at a time. The men drop to the pavement with two heavy thuds. Stepping over them, StoneFace grabs the edge of the gate, pulls it open, and waves for the rest of us to follow him.

"Who the fuck is this guy?" Liam breathes out, his gun drawn, his eyes wide with admiration.

I laugh, because StoneFace is our own personal commando. "A bad guy's worst fucking nightmare."

We file through the gate in a swarm of guns and

leather, not wasting any time, because there's no way in hell those fuckers didn't hear those shots.

There isn't a soul outside, but a few of Liam's men spread out, rounding the building, guns drawn.

StoneFace approaches the door, looks back at Judge, and waits for the rest of us catch up. A couple seconds later, Judge gives him a nod. StoneFace lifts his massive booted foot and kicks the metal door open, ripping the latch right from the jamb and bending the metal frame.

The Screwballs are ready for us this time, their guns at the ready, all pointing at the door. GP had gotten grazed from this exact same move the other day, so this time, we stand aside as bullets fly at us, pinging off the doorframe and chipping the pavement on this side of the door.

As soon as the bastards stop to reload, StoneFace barrels inside like Goliath on a mission. Liam and I are right behind him, not willing to let anyone else get to Alan before we do.

StoneFace takes out the two men closest to the door, ignoring the screams of the two naked women by the stripper pole. I don't stop to look, my eyes scanning the room in search of Alan and Big Dick.

Big Dick is nearly to the back door when StoneFace shoots him in the leg. He screams, his body arching as he drops to the ground, his hands covering the wound in his calf.

"Behind the bar," TK hollers, pushing past me, heading straight for Big Dick.

I look toward the bar, and there he is. He's not cowering like I thought he'd be. Instead, he's glaring, the barrel of his gun pressed against Tammy's temple.

"Back the fuck off or I'll shoot her," he roars.

I don't even know what else is going on in the room anymore. My focus is all on him as I cross the room in just a few strides. "Then shoot," I tell him, reaching the side of the bar.

His face twists with anger and frustration, the gun biting into Tammy's skin and drawing blood. "I'm fucking serious!"

I glance at Tammy, who looks utterly terrified, and once again, I'm left to question my own faith, because her fear doesn't bother me at all. Tammy is just as vile as the rest of these assholes, and if he actually did pull the trigger, he'd be doing the world a favor.

"Please," she pleads, tears flowing down her cheeks.

"Looks like time's up, Tammy."

Growling, Alan shoves Tammy to the floor and swings around, his gun moving toward me. I reach across the bar and wrap my hand around his wrist before he makes it all the way around.

Liam is right beside me. As Alan attempts to pull away, he rears back and brings the butt of his own gun down on top of Alan's head. His hand going slack,

Alan drops the gun and falls to the floor behind the bar.

"That him?" Liam asks.

Nodding, I jump over the bar top and land with my feet on either side of Alan. Tammy screams again and scrambles back, desperate to get away.

Paying her no mind, I grab Alan by the collar of his shirt and drag him around to the open floor in front of the bar. He doesn't move a muscle. Out cold.

I look up, taking in the scene around me. It's chaos. We may not have caught these fuckers off guard, but we outnumber them three to one. Several of their guys are on the ground, a collective pool of blood spreading across the tiles.

Leaning over Alan, Liam snarls, "Wake up, mother-fucker," repeatedly smacking his cheek.

Alan's eyelids flutter, and when his vision comes into focus, he reaches out, searching for his gun.

"Looking for this?" I ask, waving the gun in the air.

Alan gapes up at me, still dazed.

"You the fucker that treated my sister like a fucking sex doll?" Liam sneers, pressing his foot down on top of Alan's hand.

Alan hisses in pain, his face twisted with anger, making him look even more vile. "I don't even know your sister."

"I believe you called her Boo?"

His face goes from angry to terrified. "Collins? Boo is a Collins?"

I hate him even thinking about her, let alone saying that vile name he'd given her and used every time he raped her. He doesn't deserve to have her beautiful face in his mind. He doesn't deserve to share the same fucking planet as her.

"Bria," Liam clarifies, "is *the* Collins. She's the grand-daughter of the man who started the Atlantic City Syndicate, and she's my fucking sister."

Alan closes his eyes in defeat. He's a dead man, and he knows it.

"Where's the man you bought her from?" Liam demands. "What is his name?"

"I don't fucking know," he proclaims. "It was some old pervert that owed us money."

Liam leans all the way over, his face hovering above Alan's. "What. Is. His. Name?"

"I don't know!" he cries.

"Maybe this prick can help." TK approaches us from behind and tosses Big Dick onto the floor next to Alan. "Might as well get something useful out of him before I blow his fucking nuts off."

"Fuck you," Big Dick spits from between his tattered lips. TK had already done a number on him, but men like Big Dick will never give up. They'll never accept defeat. It has to be forced upon them.

The hatred I feel for these two men burns hot in my veins. I've never liked the idea of hate. Hate is something that knits itself into the fibers of your soul and eats away at it like a cancer. But these men? I'm willing to lose a bit of my soul to take them out. I'd lose it all.

TK's patience with Big Dick has come to an end. This man has raped TK's woman, fathered her child, stalked her and the boy, and threatened their safety. TK has come to blows with him in the past, but this time is the last time. He's had enough.

Stepping around the pair on the floor, TK's heavy boot comes down on Big Dick's greasy ponytail, pinning his head to the floor, and points his pistol at his groin. I cringe a little at the idea of being shot in that particular place.

"Answer the question, or Big Dick's little dick is going to get blown off."

Alan watches this exchange through wide eyes, but he doesn't offer to give up the information we need.

"Fuck y—"

TK pulls back the hammer. "One."

Big Dick struggles, yanking on his ponytail, trying to desperately remove it from under TK's foot.

"Two."

"Listen, I—"

"Three—"

"He's dead!" Alan screams. "He's been dead for years."

TK drops the gun, but even Big Dick looks at him in surprise. "What do you mean he's dead?" Big Dick asks.

Alan sighs. "He came back a few years ago. He had the money to get Boo back, but Boo is mine, so I arranged a meetup to exchange the money for her. But instead, I killed him and dumped him in the foothills."

"You son of a bitch," Big Dick snarls, still unable to lift his head. "What did you do with the money?"

Alan swallows, unable to look his president in the eye. "I bought myself that new Harley."

Big Dick lunges for him, but he doesn't get far before his hair brings him up short. "You selfish prick!" he roars. "You betrayed your own fucking club over a bit of pussy?"

Liam's boot collides with Big Dick's jaw, and blood sprays from the impact of his kick. As he turns his head back to face us, I can tell it's broken. One side is higher than the other, and he can't seem to open his mouth anymore.

"You watch how you talk about her," Liam says, his voice much calmer than his action. Then his eyes swing to Alan. "You really kill that old fuck?"

Ripping his gaze away from Big Dick's ruined face, Alan nods.

Liam looks over at me and points down at Alan. "You want to kill him, or do you want me to?"

Alan's eyes plead with mine, tears freely flowing down his cheeks. The same way Bria had likely pled with him so many times as he violated and broke her down. I want to be the one to rid the world of his evil, but Liam is Bria's big brother.

"Do it together?" Reaching for Alan's hair, I yank him up until he's sitting on the floor with his back to the front of the bar.

Liam considers my offer. Shrugging, he places his gun at Alan's right temple. "On three?"

I lift my gun, pressing it against Alan's left temple. His body trembles uncontrollably, a wet stain spreading across the front of his jeans.

"One," Liam counts, taking a page out of TK's playbook.

"For the love of God, you're a goddamn priest!" Alan screeches.

I laugh. "I never finished seminary. Two."

"Please!" he cries.

"Three." Liam and I say it together, our eyes locked on each other's as we pull our triggers. Alan's body jolts, then slumps forward, forever silenced, and unable to hurt another human being again.

I look up to find a few of the guys ushering a group of very young and battered women from the hall in the back. When my eyes meet Judge's, he gives me the thumbs up. We got them. All of them.

All of them, except Big Dick.

Big Dick stares at Alan's body, his face an immovable mask of terror, his jaw slightly askew from the kick to the face. He realizes that this is the end. His eyes dart from TK to me. "You don't have to do this," he says, his voice garbled and thick. "God will never forgive you for killing me and the rest of these people. You know where murderers end up."

I smirk. "Then I guess we'll continue this when we meet in hell."

TK kneels in front of him, holding the gun to the underside of Big Dick's chin. "Harrison will never even know your name," he vows. "All he will ever know is that the man that fathered him was a sack of shit rapist, and that I blew his fucking brains out."

A lone tear escapes Big Dick's eye and races down his cheek, but he holds TK's gaze, defiant and proud. "He's still my so—"

Blood and brains spray the bar behind him before he can finish his sentence.

"He was never your fucking son," TK growls before rearing back and kicking him in the face for good measure.

Silence falls as we take in the bloodbath. Every single

member of the Screwballs MC is dead. They won't be trafficking or torturing any more innocent women.

"What do you say we get home to our ladies?" Judge says, pulling a wrinkled handkerchief from the pocket of his jeans. He smooths it out and uses it to wipe the spray of blood from his cheeks, but his smile is filled with relief. "I need a drink."

Chapter 28

BRIA

I'M wide awake when the rumble of motorcycles grows louder outside. Whipping back the blankets, I bolt from Priest's bed, not stopping to check my appearance. The need to see him safe outweighs the need to look presentable. The need to tell him everything.

The other ladies are already in the main room when Judge comes through the front door. Grace runs to him, clutching him in her arms. Judge leans down and kisses her, grinning as one by one, the others file inside. Some of them look worse off than others, but when Priest walks into the room, my heart stops.

He's safe. He's alive. He's come back to me.

I don't think, I just run. I run to the man I love, slamming into him without even attempting to apply brakes. My mouth goes straight for his, ignoring the catcalling crowd around us, and the disapproving eye of my brother standing behind him. I ignore Liam when he clears his throat, taking solace in the warmth of Priest's arms. I'm surrounded by the scent of his body wash. That comforting mixture of sandalwood and spice I've grown to cherish on his pillow.

"You're okay?" I step back, running my hands over his body, inspecting every inch of him. No bullet or stab wounds.

"I'm fine, Angel," he assures me, pulling me in for another kiss. Passion ripples from his full lips to mine, want and need tugging at us both. "It's done."

I pull away and stare at him. "Done?"

Liam steps up beside us and nods. "They're dead. All of them."

"Alan?"

"We took care of him together, Angel," Priest informs me, kissing the back of my hand. "He will never hurt you or anyone else again."

I want to know what happened. I want to know the details of how he died. But in truth, knowing he's gone is enough. Relief floods my chest, fresh air filling my lungs for what feels like the first time in so very long. *I'm free. I'm finally free.*

I peer over Priest's shoulder and meet Liam's gaze. There's blood splatter all across his face and body. His crisp white shirt will never be white again, and the suit jacket he'd been wearing is gone.

"Liam, are you okay?" I slide from Priest's arms and around him until I reach my brother, worry squeezing my heart all over again. I run my hands over him, checking him for wounds as well.

Liam laughs, his hands coming up to rest on my shoulders. "It's not mine, Bebe. I'm fine. You don't have to mother me. Though I must admit, seeing your concern warms my heart."

I crinkle my nose, not sure if he's teasing me or not. "You're my brother. I'm going to care if you get hurt."

"Glad to hear it." He smiles, but there's pain behind that smile. We've lost so much time together. Time we can never get back. Liam shifts, clearly uncomfortable with the heaviness of the moment. "Oh, we brought you a gift."

"A gift?"

Liam calls to someone outside. The door swings open, and dozens of women are being ushered inside.

"Told you we'd get them out," Priest whispers into my ear as he moves up behind me. He pulls my back to his chest as the women walk into the room, their eyes wide and uncertain. Some have open wounds. Others are a little worse for wear, but it's the woman in the middle of the group that obliterates my happiness.

Tammy.

That conniving bitch made it out, though not in good condition. Her hair is bloody and matted to her head.

Her clothes are tattered. She scans the room until her eyes land on me. Relief grows on her face as she starts for me. As she draws closer, she opens her arms, attempting to embrace me, but before she can reach me, I step away.

Evil Tammy doesn't miss a beat. "Oh my God, Boo, you're alive!" she squeals. "I'm so happy to see you."

"That makes one of us," I say, glaring at her. I hate that she's here in this place I've found safety in. I hate that she's invading my newfound happiness. And who the hell does she think she's fooling by acting like we're friends?

Liam watches, his brow furrowing at the change in my tone. He studies me for a moment and asks, "Aren't you happy with your gift, Bebe?"

Priest squeezes me tighter as I force myself to answer. "I am."

Liam isn't buying it. "Then explain your tone."

I consider my words, my eyes boring into Tammy. I don't look away when I say, "Not all of these women are good. Some tortured us more than the men. Not all of them are victims. They made my life hell."

"Who are they?" Liam growls, whipping around to stare at the group. "Point them out."

The blood drains from Tammy's face, her guilt too much to hide.

I could conceal my hatred for this woman, but why? After everything she's put me and these other women through, why should I spare her? She'd beaten me. She'd battered so many girls that had come along. She'd laughed at us and lied to the MC to make them punish us, all for the sake of jealousy. She doesn't deserve my mercy.

I hold her terrified stare and point directly at her. "Her."

I then point out two other women, Sarah and Mary. Both had helped Tammy setup the new girls, but Mary had been sent away not long after she arrived as a gift to another one of their chapters. How she ended up back with the mother chapter, I'll never know, but she's here, and so is Sarah, the snitch. The one who lived to stir up trouble, and she was Tammy's second-in-command. Sarah had helped Tammy poison Jozie, and then helped her cover it up.

None of these three women were innocent. They had just as much blood on their hands as the Screwballs did. They'd just had less power. They'd done horrible things, and it was time for them to be held accountable.

"Grab them," Liam orders. Three members of the Syndicate move as soon as the words leave his mouth. Sarah and Mary fall back, attempting to hide themselves in the center of the group, but there's no escaping this fate. "Bring them to me."

I watch, my emotions swirling with shame and fear, wondering if I've made the right choice. The ladies are brought to stand in front of Liam, all of them trembling under my brother's anger.

Liam retrieves the gun from his holster and holds it out to me. "Kill them. Show them what happens when you fuck with a Collins."

I stare at the gun, my conscience unable to settle on what's right and wrong here.

"You don't have to do this, sweetheart," Priest whispers behind me. "Whatever decision you make, I won't judge you. Just consider all the options."

Judge joins the group, his brows lifting when he sees the gun Liam is offering me. "I take it I missed something?"

"These three cunts tortured my sister."

"I see," Judge mutters, frowning. He doesn't argue with Liam, nor does he stop me when I reach for the gun. My hands tremble as they draw near it. This is my chance to get the revenge I had dreamed of against these bitches. Revenge not only for me, but for all the other women they'd messed with.

My fingertips graze the cool metal, but that touch has me dropping my hand to my side. "I won't kill them."

Sighing, Liam nods and places the gun back in its holster. He doesn't approve, but he doesn't argue with my decision.

"If I kill them, I'm no better than they are. They had a

choice, just like I did. I just happened to make the right one."

Liam's disapproval fades from those green eyes of his, replaced with understanding. He steps forward, leans into me, and places a kiss to my forehead. It's the first show of affection we've shared, and I know in that moment, I will love my brother until the end of forever. He's supporting me, and he'll do what I can't.

"It appears my sister is more merciful than I am," he declares, turning to face Tammy and the others. Mary releases a sigh of relief, and Sarah's shoulders relax. But Liam is quick to hold up his hand for their attention. "Don't get ahead of yourselves, ladies. I never said my sister's mercy has anything to do with what I plan to do with you."

"We were just as trapped as she was," Tammy cries. "We're victims too."

"Victims?" I huff, her plea hitting me like a slap in the face. Moving from the comfort of Priest's arms, I storm toward the three of them. "You were never a victim, Tammy. None of you were." I make sure to look each one of them in the eye as I speak. "My decision wasn't based on mercy. Mercy isn't something I would ever give any of you. But I do have the self-respect to know that killing you won't matter. You mean nothing to me. Your lives mean nothing to anyone, and they will continue to mean nothing while I have everything."

Tammy's eyes flash with hatred and fear.

"Fear is a good look for you, Tammy. It'll do you well with what comes next."

"What comes next?" she asks, her voice rising an octave.

Liam steps forward, putting us shoulder to shoulder. Well, it would be if his height wasn't dwarfing mine. "You're lucky you've caught me in a good mood, ladies. I'm feeling rather generous, so I'll tell you what. I'll give you a one-hour head start. My sister may not want to kill you, but me?" He grins. "I'm a whole new kind of monster."

"An hour for what?" Mary sobs.

Liam narrows his eyes. "To run. One hour, then I'm coming to find you. And when I find you, you'll wish Bria had just shot you here and been done with it."

The women look at each other, unsure of what to do. I almost feel sorry for them. Almost.

Liam peers down to the watch on his wrist. "Tick tock, ladies. You're wasting precious time."

Their feet move, tripping over each other as they run, desperate to escape before another second ticks away. Liam's men step aside, and Judge gives a nod of approval to let them leave out the back door.

"That was certainly interesting," Judge chuckles. "What's your plan for when the hour's up?"

Liam's face splits into a grin, rivaled only by the Cheshire cat. "I have a few ideas."

"Remind me never to piss him off," TK mutters.

Karma laughs and looks at Judge. "What do you want to do with the others? These ladies are exhausted and waiting for their marching orders."

"Call Doc. They need medical care. They can use the spare rooms for now. Have the ladies help them get cleaned up. I'll send Burnt and V out to get extra supplies, and whatever else we need for them."

"And after that?" I ask.

Judge's eyes go soft when he turns to me. "We help them find their families. If they don't have family, we help them start over. Their suffering ends here."

The ladies of the club immediately get to work, shuttling the women into one room or the next, while Cora and Grace head straight for the kitchen.

As the room clears, Liam moves to walk away, but I reach out, grasping his arm. Pushing up on my tiptoes, I plant a kiss on his cheek. "Thank you for letting me make that call. I know you didn't have to, but you did anyway."

"Wasn't my call to make, Bebe." He taps me on the nose and smiles. "Think I'll go get myself cleaned up."

"You can use my room," Priest offers.

Liam grimaces. "The fuck I will. I saw what you were doing to my sister in there."

Priest barks out a laugh. "Fair enough."

"We have a couple of hotel rooms booked nearby," Liam offers. "We'll get cleaned up and be back in the morning. You'll be ready by then?" His question is aimed at me, catching me off guard.

His business here is finished, and now that the threat is gone, he intends to follow through on his promise to take me home.

Liam doesn't wait for my answer. Instead, with a wave of his hand, he signals his men to follow him as he exits.

"What did he mean by 'you'll be ready'?" Priest asks. Turning to him, I wrap my arms around his waist, drawing him close. "What's going on?" he asks again.

"Take me away, Priest. Take me away from here."

Studying my face, he gives me a smile that steals my breath away. "With pleasure, Angel. With fucking pleasure."

PRIEST

I ROLL OVER, my heart still racing as I try to catch my breath. I've made love to Bria every available chance we've had these past few days we've been away. When she asked me to take her away, I did. We traveled to the coast and found a tiny Airbnb on the water. We've been taking the time to get to know each other and enjoy each other's company. I swear, I can't get enough of this woman.

My phone buzzes on the table, the ringer silent. Judge again. He's been blowing up my phone since the moment we took off. After what happened the last time I left the safety of the club, I'm sure he's pissed, but I'm not ready to answer to him yet. I'm not ready for him to call me back to the clubhouse.

Liam has also been calling. If Judge is pissed, Liam's irate. If the voicemails he's left me are any indication, he's got a bullet in the chamber of his gun with my name on it. He's convinced I've kidnapped his sister before he could finally get her back, and he's not going to let that slide.

Bria rolls onto her side and places a hand on my chest. "Liam again?"

I shake my head. "Judge. Says I need to get my ass back there."

Sighing, she slides over me, tucking her naked body against the side of mine. "Maybe we should go."

I look down at her, sliding my fingers through her hair. "You want to?"

"Not really. I love being here with you, but at the same time, I've just found out I have a brother, and he wants to get to know me. I want to get to know him too, but..."

I wait for her to continue, but she doesn't. "But what, Angel?"

A blush creeps into her cheeks. "But I don't want to leave you."

Thank God. "I'm not leaving you, Angel. Not for a second. I'll be here for as long as you'll have me."

"Really?"

I frown, not liking the doubt I hear in her tone. "Baby, I'm not trying to pressure you into anything you're not ready for. I know you've been through hell, and I can't imagine the trauma you have to heal before you feel whole again. But if you'll let me, I want to be there with you every fucking step of the way."

Bria swallows, a tear escaping and sliding down her freckled cheek. "I don't know if I can do that without you."

I tip my head to the side. "Angel, you could. I don't want you to, but you can fucking do anything, with or without me. You're the bravest woman I've ever met." She closes her eyes and shakes her head. "Baby, look at me."

She opens her eyes, her lashes now wet with tears, but she doesn't say a word as she holds my stare.

"You've been through a hell most men couldn't handle. You stayed strong, you stayed true to who you are, and you never fucking broke. If that isn't strength, I don't know what is."

Bria chokes back a sob and cups my cheek. "I love you," she whispers.

My heart misses three whole beats as I take in her timid smile, and that's when I know. I know that I can't live without this woman. Yes, I'd absolutely done it before I met her, but was that really living? Because since I met Bria, my life has been filled with color and love. Yes, I love her. I just hadn't wanted to tell her that before she was ready and risk scaring her away.

"Marry me," I say, sliding up on the mattress until my back is against the headboard.

Bria sits up, blinking at me in surprise. "What?"

"You heard me, Angel. Marry me."

She clutches the blankets to her chest, a tiny frown forming on her brow. "But we hardly know each other."

Reaching for her hand, I pull it to my chest, splaying her palm over my heart. "I know you snore," I say, grinning when she gasps. "I know you like peanut butter on your toast and three sugars in your coffee. I know you love children and are good with Henley. I know you like to hum in the shower, and you sleep on your side, rolled up like a fucking armadillo. I know that we still have a lot of moments from our pasts we haven't yet shared with each other, but since you came along, mine doesn't seem to cast a cloud of darkness over me anymore. It can't, because you light up everything around you."

Tears flow freely down Bria's cheeks, her eyes filled with so much love and tenderness. "Priest," she whispers.

"I love you, Angel. I love you so fucking much, it hurts to breathe sometimes. I want to be the one at your back when you make the hard choices. I want to protect you from the nastiness of the world so it can never touch you again. I want to help you heal and conquer this whole damn universe, because I can't imagine a life without you in it. You deserve to be loved, Angel. You deserve to be shown kindness, love, and respect. Let me do that for you. Let me be the one to give you all of that. Marry me."

She stares at me for longer than I'm comfortable with. When she finally moves, she throws herself forward, colliding with my chest and feathering kisses all over my face. "Yes," she sobs. "Yes, I'll marry you."

Relief washes over me. My decision to ask her may not have been planned, but just the idea of her saying no is enough to crush me. "I swear I'll make you happy, Angel."

"You already do." Her lips move to mine, claiming them in a slow, tender kiss.

When she pulls away, I grin, feeling almost giddy with joy. "Come on." Flipping back the covers, I jump out of bed and tug on my jeans.

"Where are we going?"

"To get married," I reply, digging in the dresser for a clean shirt.

Bria stands, her head tipped to the side. "Now?"

The shirt I'm looking for is at the bottom of the pile. Pulling it out, I turn to her as I slide it over my head. "Absolutely."

"But… we don't even have rings."

"We'll buy them. I'll buy you a huge one." Picking her sundress off the floor, I toss it to her. "Baby, get dressed. I won't sleep until you have my last name."

She pulls on the dress and giggles, clearly thinking I'm crazy. "I don't even *know* your last name."

She's right. I don't even think she knows my first name. "Russo." I reach out my hand to her. "Mateo Russo."

Giggling, she puts her hand in mine, grinning from ear to ear. "Nice to meet you, Mateo."

I turn her around, giving her a pat on the butt. "Nice to meet you too. Now go, get ready. We've got a wedding to go to."

BRIA

TWO WEEKS LATER

Priest approaches the gate and pulls up next to the guard shack. A beast of a man steps from the booth, the gun at his hip on full display. "State your business."

I lean across the center console, straining my neck to see him as I speak. "I'm Bria Collins. I'm here to see my brother, Liam. Can you let him know I'm here?"

The man leans down and peers into our rental car, then huffs. His hand goes to his earpiece, and he says something into the receiver on his chest. The metal gate in front of us clicks heavily as it unlocks and creaks open.

"Go straight on to the main house. Mr. Collins will meet you there."

"Thanks," Priest mutters before driving through the gate, which promptly closes behind us. "He's certainly spared no expense on security."

"No shit," I say, looking around at the opulence of Liam's estate. Priest drives up the winding driveway until the house comes into full view. I gasp when I see it.

"Think it's big enough?" Priest jokes as we draw closer.

The enormous property sits on the edge of the Atlantic Ocean. White siding contrasts beautifully against the cool blue hues of the ocean behind it. Large windows span the length of five separate floors. There must be perfect views of the ocean and the open property around it from inside.

"Wonder how much all this privacy cost him. Ocean-front property has to be at a premium around here."

"I don't even want to think about how much this house cost," I admit. My brother has money, clearly. The expensive suits I'd seen him wear was a clue to his financial status, but this house? I didn't expect this at all. I envisioned an older family home, passed down from our grandfather upon his death. This home is new and modern, and the epitome of wealth.

The ornate front doors open as Priest brings the car to a stop. Liam steps out, wearing a designer suit, of course. He certainly has a good sense of style. Even after he stayed a week back in Austin, he wore a new suit every day. All business all the time, it seems with him.

"Bria," he greets, opening my door for me. Helping

me out of the car, I step into the sunny coastal air with a smile. "Welcome home."

"Thanks," I breathe.

Priest rounds the SUV and joins us, shaking my brother's hand firmly. Liam's eyes are narrowed as he looks at my husband. He had argued about Priest coming with me, but I'd put my foot down, telling him that where I go, Priest goes. Little does my brother know that there's another reason he's with me. I just have to hope that news will be better received than my request for him to join us.

"Let's get you inside." Liam places his hand on my lower back and ushers me up the steps.

His home is larger inside than it appears. Each room is an open concept style, with few walls separating off the spaces. Minimalist furniture and adornments decorate the space. A fancy bachelor's pad. One created for function instead of beauty. A space lacking a woman's touch.

"Do you like it?"

"It's big, I'll give you that." My eyes don't know what to look at first. I don't remember ever seeing a place so luxurious. "This is really where we grew up?"

He shrugs. "More or less. I've renovated it quite a bit, but it's still home."

I try to imagine what it would've been like growing up here. All these rooms to play in, and never having to worry about where my next meal was going to come from. The life of privilege I'd been denied. A life that even I question, wondering if it would've been a version of myself that I would have wanted.

"Kitchen is there." With a point of his index finger, he indicates a white marble kitchen with matching white cabinets. "Dining room is there. My office is just behind the kitchen, and the living room is over there, with one of the best views in all of Atlantic City." He points out each space with a hopeful smile.

"And our room?"

"I have your room up on the top floor with mine. There's an elevator. One of my housekeeper's will get your luggage taken up and unpacked." He turns his gaze to Priest. "I have you in the guest suite on the second floor."

I crinkle my nose. "He's staying with me."

"Not under my roof," Liam growls.

Frustration takes over. These past couple of weeks with Priest have taught me that I don't answer to anyone, even my older brother. "I've been here five minutes, and you're already growling at me, Liam. How are we going to get through a few weeks together if you can't even acknowledge my wishes?"

"What is that supposed to mean?" he argues. "I won't allow you to share a room with any man under my roof. Not even *him*."

God, he's so infuriating! Well, I'll fix that.

"It's only fitting that my husband sleeps with his wife," I say, narrowing my eyes at him.

Liam's body goes rigid. I can almost see the steam coming out of his ears with the news I so casually dropped on him. I had initially planned to tell him about our wedding at dinner tonight, but his insistence on us sleeping separately is outdated and absurd. Priest side-eyes me, a sigh escaping his thin lips. I shrug an apology to him, but it had to be done.

"What do you mean married?" Liam's angry glare darts to Priest. "You fucking married my sister?" he roars. "Married my sister without my permission?"

Priest nods. "I did."

"How fucking dare you!" Liam charges Priest, but I step in the way, just in time to stop the collision.

Placing a hand on his chest, I stare up at my brother, holding firm as I say, "I'm not some possession you own, Liam. You don't get to decide who I can and cannot marry. I'm a grown woman, and can make my own decisions just fine. And I choose Priest. He's my choice."

Liam's chest heaves up and down, his face growing redder by the minute. He looks between us both before throwing up his hand in an exasperated growl. "My office, now. It appears we need to have a talk sooner rather than I'd planned."

He stomps off in a huff toward another part of the house, expecting me to follow him.

"That could've gone better, Angel," my husband whispers from behind me.

"It could have, but I'll be damned if I'm going to be separated from you. He'll cool down."

Priest arches his brow. "And if he doesn't?"

Shrugging, I flash him a smile. "Atlantic City honeymoon?"

Priest chuckles and shakes his head. "You may not remember him, but I dare say you do know how to push his buttons. I'll see if I can find our room while you go talk with your brother. Let me know if I need to toss our bags over the railings and make a run for it." With a kiss to my forehead, Priest heads off in the opposite direction of where Liam went. Hopefully he's putting as much distance as he can between the two of them.

"Now, Bria!" Liam bellows from down the hall. With a sigh, I head toward his voice until I find an open door. Peering around the edge of the frame, I spy my brother, pacing back and forth inside. His office, I suspect, has a large desk, and an expansive library takes up three of the four walls. A portrait of our family hangs on the other, right in the center behind the desk. "Close the door," he orders.

Bristling at his orders, I do what he says. Cautiously, I

walk into his domain like prey trying to avoid the predator.

"Why didn't you tell me you married him?"

"It didn't seem like something you'd want to hear over the phone, Liam." Not that I knew how to work the fancy phone Hashtag had given me anyway. The thing had so many bells, whistles, and buttons, that outside of hitting the call button and texting, I'm at a loss as to what to do with it. I've never even had an email address or an ID card, let alone a cell phone. "I love him, Liam. And besides, I thought you'd be happy I married a priest."

"Former priest," Liam throws back at me. "How much do you even know about this man, Bria? You just met him."

"The amount of time I've known him doesn't matter. It matters here," I say, pressing my finger against my chest. "My soul knows his. What we've been through, it's forged an unbreakable connection." Liam growls again. "If you keep doing that growling thing, you'll be hoarse in no time," I tease, hoping to diffuse the tension in the room.

Liam continues pacing, dangerously close to getting on my last nerve. Unable to continue to watch him, I move toward him, stepping into his path. "Look at me, Liam. I mean, really look at me. I'm happy with him.

Why can't you share the same joy I feel, knowing that for the first time in my life, I'm actually happy?"

"I wanted so much more for you than the life of a biker's wife. After everything…" He pauses. "After everything that's happened to you, I wanted this to be your new lease on life. A chance to see the world for the good in it rather than the darker side." Liam grows quiet. His gaze shifts to the portrait behind his desk. "I feel like I've failed them, our parents. I should've been able to keep you safe."

"Liam, you were a child. We both were. What matters now is that you found me." I step forward, closing the distance between us. I reach out and pull his hand into mine. "Life hasn't been easy for either of us, but this is our chance. The chance for both of us to be happy."

He considers that for a moment, his jaw ticking as he thinks. Then, pulling me against him in a tight embrace, he says, "I don't want to lose you again, Bebe."

"You won't," I promise. "Just because I'm living in Austin, doesn't mean I can't come visit. And the same goes for you. Judge gave you an open invitation, I'm told, and I expect you to use it."

Liam gazes down at me, eyes filled with a mixture of happy and sad, something I'm all too familiar with. After a moment, he frowns, his eyes zeroing in on my hand still in his. "Where's your wedding ring?"

"We haven't exactly gotten around to picking one out yet," I admit.

Liam stares at me and nods, saying nothing. I watch as he drops my hand and turns, walking toward the enormous portrait. He touches the edge and the frame swings wide, revealing a safe set into the wall. He presses his fingerprint against a scanner and the lock safe clicks, popping the door open. Without a word, he reaches inside, retrieving a small black box.

He moves to stand before me and takes my wrist, placing the tiny box in my palm. "Open it."

Confused, I peer down at the box and do as he asks. Gently, I open the lid and gasp when I see what's inside.

A beautiful vintage ring set in platinum, with black geometric diamonds flanking a large diamond stone in the middle, sits nestled in a velvet cushion. The center stone glitters beneath the lights of the room. A dazzling brilliance of colors.

"What is this?"

"That was our grandmother's wedding ring. The same one our mum wore when she married Da."

"Liam," I breathe. "I can't accept this. This is too much."

Plucking the ring from the box, he takes my hand and slide the heirloom onto my bare finger. When his eyes lift to mine, he smiles. "This was always meant to be yours, Bebe. I'm just glad I get the chance to see you wear it."

"It's beautiful," I say, unable to look away as the reflection of the ocean catches on the center stone. "Does this mean I have your blessing?"

Liam cocks his brow. "A little late for that."

I giggle. "True. But having it would mean the world to me."

"Priest is not who I would've picked for you, Bria, but I know he can protect you. His club will protect you. A man who is willing to kill to protect what he loves is a man I can come to call my brother-in-law. In due time, of course."

"Of course." I try and fail to hold back my smirk. "Now come on. You owe me a tour of your house."

Liam shakes his head. "Our house, Bebe. Don't forget, you're a Collins too."

"Actually, I'm a former Collins," I remind him. "Though, I don't actually know my new last name." I place a finger to my chin and Liam scowls, which only makes me laugh. "Kidding, big brother. Stow your growling. I'm a Russo now."

"An Italian," Liam groans, scrubbing a hand over his face. "I think Priest and I need to have a little talk."

"Don't be too hard on him about marrying me without your permission. It truly was a spur of the moment thing, but I don't regret it. He makes me happy."

"Don't worry, Bebe. He'll get what's coming for him."

I sigh, knowing that Priest can handle whatever Liam throws at him. "That's what I'm afraid of."

The two men in my life. The brother I never knew I had, and the man I never expected to love.

This has to be what happiness looks like. And going forward, it's this happiness I'll cling to for the rest of my life.

Chapter 31

PRIEST

"YOU READY FOR THIS?" I ask, giving her hand a squeeze before we go inside. "Judge is probably gonna shoot me on the spot as soon as we walk in there."

Bria smiles. "Nah. Judge will understand. If not, I'll sic Grace on him."

I huff out a laugh. "I see you're already beginning to understand how this club operates."

Bria grins and pops up on her toes, placing a quick kiss to my lips. "Let's go. Might as well get this over with."

With a heavy sigh, I pull the door open and we step inside the clubhouse. Several of the guys are at the bar, and the women are gathered around the pool table. As soon as Judge sees me, the room falls silent. I watch as he walks toward me, his face unreadable as he approaches.

"Oh, God," Bria whispers, her fingers biting into my arm.

He comes to a stop directly in front of us. "Glad to see you've decided to come home. You planning on sticking around?"

I nod, but don't dare speak.

"You're on prospect duty for the rest of the year," he declares. "Lower than a prospect. Even the prospects can pass their shit jobs onto you, and you'll fucking do them."

It could be worse, I guess...

"Oh. My. God." Cora squeals, approaching with Grace. Cora's eyes have zeroed in on where Bria's hand squeezes my arm. It's her ring she's looking at. "You got married?" she squeals even louder.

My eyes flash to Judge's, knowing damn well he's not happy about this interruption, but my heart swells with pride as I watch Bria. Her light has never been brighter. And besides Liam, we haven't yet told a soul about our union. Cora is the first person to be equally as excited as we are about it.

Unable to hide her smile, Bria nods, holding her hand out for Cora to get a better look.

The men forgotten, Cora and Grace crowd in, commenting on the unique jewelry. Blair, Lindsey, and the others rush over, each of them congratulating me and Bria, all of them making a fuss over Bria's ring.

Originally, I hadn't been too sure about how I felt with Bria wearing a ring her brother had handed her to symbolize our marriage. But for so many years, Bria had been alone. Now she has a brother, and a past to discover. And apparently, a vintage family heirloom, the likes of which I'd never have been able to afford.

"For fuck's sake," Judge mutters behind me. He's probably pissed off because he got interrupted in the middle of ripping me a new asshole, but watching Bria, I can't seem to bring myself to care.

"Oh, stop being such an old grouch," Grace huffs, nudging him and pointing to us. "Can you think of two people who deserve this more?"

Judge stares at his wife, but doesn't answer.

Grace rolls her eyes and pulls Bria in for a hug. "Well, if he won't say it, I will. Welcome to the family, honey."

Bria's smile is radiant. "Thank you."

My heart grows fuller than it's ever been. Just a few weeks ago, she'd been alone and afraid, begging for death to carry her away from her own reality. Now she's a married woman, attached to a family filled with women who treat each other with kindness instead of jealousy.

Several members of the club move forward, shaking my hand and clapping me on the back. "You shouldn't have taken off like that," TK scolds, taking my hand and giving it a firm shake. "But I'm glad you found your happiness."

I hear Bria telling the others about our little city hall wedding, and the motorcycle adventure along the coast.

When Judge approaches Bria, I brace, worried he may say something to upset her, but I should know better. Judge may be a hard-ass, but he's a good man, and he knows how much Bria means to me.

"Darlin'," he starts. "Want you to know that I think you're a very strong woman, and I couldn't have picked a better wife for Priest. You're part of this club now. You need anything, you just ask."

"Thank you," Bria breathes out. Had she been as worried as I was?

For the next couple of hours, I watch as Bria rides the wave of well wishes. Her smile is infectious, and it's hard to believe that she'd been raped before my very eyes just over a month ago.

"Angel?" I call out once the crowd has scattered.

"Mmm?" The look on her face is one of contentment and peace. I don't ever want that look to disappear.

"Come with me." Taking her hand in mine, I lead her toward the door, anxious to get a moment to ourselves, even if it's just for a few seconds. As soon as we're outside, I back her up against the side of the building and step between her parted legs.

"You happy, Angel?"

She playfully smacks my chest and declares, "I have never been happier in my life."

I don't laugh at her light tone. Instead, I drop to my knees and take her hand, assuming the proposal position all over again. "Bria Russo, you are the most incredible person I've ever met. You've been through more in just a few short years than most people have been through in their entire lives."

Bria holds my gaze, eyes shining with unshed tears.

"I think maybe God is real after all," I admit. "I think that though he can't control the actions of evil bastards like the ones in our pasts, he can use those experiences to make us better people."

I reach into my pocket and pull out the tiny jewelry box. The white gold necklace holds a rather large diamond, surrounded by several smaller ones. It's simple and understated, but it's her. Delicate and dainty, and absolutely gorgeous.

"I know you have a ring," I say, gazing up into her questioning eyes. "But as much as I love the ring you have, I wanted to give you something from me."

"Put it on," she whispers, turning her back to me and lifting her hair away from the nape of her neck.

I struggle a little with the tiny clasp, but after a couple of attempts, I click it into place. When Bria turns, I can only stare at her.

"I believe we were made for each other," I continue,

catching a tear before it rolls too far down her cheek. "I believe all the shit we've both been through has prepared us for the life we're about to have."

"I believe that too," she whispers.

Leaning forward, I capture her lips in a soft, sensual kiss, caressing her tongue with my own. Fuck, this woman was made just for me.

"Make love to me," she breathes against my mouth.

"Right now?"

She looks around the parking lot. "Have you ever had sex on your motorcycle?"

I shake my head, pleasantly surprised by the idea. Again, more proof she was made just for me.

Bending low, I press my shoulder into her belly and stand, carrying her over my shoulder like a sack of flour.

"Where are we going?" she squeals.

"First," I say, clapping one hand down on her perfectly formed ass. "I'm going to make love to you on the seat of that motorcycle."

"Mmhmm," she murmurs.

"And then, I'm going to take you into the bedroom and lick your pussy until you forget your own name."

"Oh my," she purrs.

"You game?"

"Can I change my question?" she asks, pushing up from my shoulder so she can meet my eyes.

"Always."

"You ever licked pussy on the seat of your motorcycle?"

I shake my head, because no, I've never even thought about it. But now, that's all I want to think about.

We reach the motorcycle, and I place her feet on the ground.

"Mrs. Russo, you're a very naughty woman."

Grinning, Bria glides her shorts down her legs and kicks them off to the side. I watch as she slides her ass up onto the seat of my motorcycle and parts her knees. "I'm just in love with a beautiful man who happens to have a magical tongue."

"Fucking made for me," I mutter. And then I move in, ready to remind my wife just how magical my tongue is.

Epilogue

BURNT

"DUDE, where the fuck are you taking me?" I ask, staring up at the abandoned warehouse. "If you wanted to take me out somewhere to kill me, man, at least you could've sprung for something better than burgers and fries."

"Shut up," V growls. "It's just through here."

"What's through here, a tetanus shot?" The entire place looks like it's about to cave in. The roof has holes big enough for a Buick to fall through.

"You're making me regret bringing you along. You know that, right?"

"Well, when you promised me a night of fucking debauchery away from the club, I didn't think it would be this." I wave at the building in front of us. "Seriously, if this is your idea of fun, you need to find a new hobby."

V glares back at me from over his shoulder. "Just follow me."

"To my death," I mutter under my breath.

We walk until we come to a cellar door at the far end of the building. V leans down, knocks four times, then stands back.

"Is this when the serial killer in a clown mask comes out asking if I float?"

"Stay out here then, asshole, but my ass is going in there to see what this place is all about."

"Tetanus. That's what's in there."

A few minutes go by before a heavy metal clang comes from the other side of the door. It swings wide, revealing a woman wearing nothing but a scrap of gauzy sheer fabric. Crossing her tattooed arms over the perkiest set of tits I've seen in a while, she utters, "Password."

"Blueberry pancakes," V replies.

The sexy as hell woman licks her lips and grins as she steps aside, giving us room to enter.

"Welcome to Vanilla Villa. Please, follow me."

V shoots me a warning look before following the woman down the stairs. The metal cellar door slams behind us, and my senses blur from the sudden lack of light. The deeper we go, the more my heart races.

"You sure about this place?" I whisper to V. But even in a whisper, the sound of my voice echoes off the walls.

"Jesus, man. Say it a little louder."

The clacking heels of the woman's shoes comes to a stop, and I almost smack right into V's back.

I hear the party before I see it, the thumping base of the music slipping through the crack of the door behind her. The woman knocks on something I can't see and the door opens, light filling the space, revealing the crowd inside.

"Holy fucking shit," I breathe, my eyes wide. This is definitely not grandma's cellar. The entire place is filled to the brim with people. Some are dancing, some are talking. Some are fucking right there in plain view of everyone else. Something brushes past my head. I crane my neck and find women suspended from the ceiling, with ball gags in their mouths.

"Told you," V throws back at me.

"Dude, this is like fucking adult Disneyland." I grab his shoulder, shaking the fucking shit out of it.

"This is just the first room. Come on," he beckons. "The good shit is in the back."

"How the fuck did you find out about this place?"

"One of Liam's guys."

We weave through the crowd, stopping when two women slide in between us, their tits covered in cum. Clearly, they'd already had some fun tonight. Shit, who knew how many rounds these women had gone through already. They looked as if the circle jerk party had started at their house. Getting my dick wet is why I came along, catching something isn't.

"Hey, handsome. You wanna play?" cum tits asks, her voice sultry and flirty. "You look like you would fuck very hard."

V grins as her friend presses against him, whispering in his ear. I side-eye V, shrugging my shoulders. He shakes his head no, and whispers something to the girl plastered to him. Sneering, she grabs her friend and stalks off into the crowd.

"The fuck did you tell them?"

"You don't wanna know. Liam's guy warned me about some of the girls. If they have a red bracelet on, they're looking to peg. You don't strike me as a guy who likes something being shoved up his ass."

Jesus. What is this place? "You'd be correct."

"Come on. There're some private rooms toward the back. More our speed, I think."

We continue on through more sweaty bodies before coming to a halt where two guards stand with a velvet red rope spanning the space between them. The big guy stares at us, his face void of any expression. Slipping his hand into his back pocket, V pulls out a black card and hands it to him. The guy nods, unclips the rope between them, and allows us to pass.

A row of rooms line the hallway behind the rope. Every

single door is wide open, revealing couples and groups of people fucking loudly inside. The sound of slapping bodies and moans fill the hallway. V moves on ahead of me, but one open door in particular catches my eye. I skid to a stop, grabbing V by the shoulder to halt his forward pursuit.

"The fuck?" he groans, but his protests stop when he notices what's caught my eye.

Inside this room, a woman sits in a high-backed leather chair, her face hidden by a black leather mask. Her long, dark hair cascades down her narrow shoulders, falling just short of her bountiful tits.

She sits in that chair like a fucking queen on a throne, her naked body on display for any who pass. I lick my lips as I take her in. Tattoos cover nearly every inch of her skin, swirls of colors and designs flowing seamlessly together. A dragon on her abdomen circles around her hips and onto her thighs.

She's a fucking goddess, ready for someone to worship her.

"Hello, there," she purrs, her sultry voice beckoning to me like a siren's song.

"Hello, beautiful," V replies, stepping through the doorway. "All alone?"

"Seems that way." She sighs. "Never seen you two around before." Ah. She's a regular, it appears. With the kind of confidence that oozes from her, it's not surprising. "First time?"

V leans up against the doorframe, crossing his tattooed arms over his chest. "Might be."

"What about your friend?" she asks, her eyes barely visible under her black mask. But I can feel them on me, the heat of her gaze going straight to my fucking cock.

"First-timer."

"Well, then, why don't you two join me? I'll give you a proper welcome to the Vanilla Villa." She uncrosses her legs, baring her bald pussy. "No one has piqued my interest tonight, but I think the two of you will serve me quite well."

V looks at me, his eyes narrowed with uncertainty. We've never shared a woman at the same time. Sure, most of the unattached guys have shared the available girls at the club, but this is different. I'm a territorial bastard. Sharing has never been a great virtue of mine.

"Didn't come all this way not to enjoy ourselves," V suggests, raising his brow.

"Fuck it," I growl. "Let's do this."

———

Read more about Burnt and V's story in Dark Seduction.

THE SERIES

Avelyn Paige is a USA Today and Wall Street Journal bestselling author who writes stories about dirty alpha males and the brave women who love them. She resides in a small town in Indiana with her husband and three fuzzy kids, Jezebel, Cleo, and Asa.

Avelyn spends her days working as a cancer research scientist and her nights sipping moonshine while writing. You can often find her curled up with a good book surrounded by her pets or watching one of her favorite superhero movies for the billionth time. Deadpool is currently her favorite.

———

Want to talk books? Join Avelyn's Facebook group to learn about new releases, future series, and to hang out with other readers.

ALSO BY AVELYN PAIGE

The Heaven's Rejects MC Series

Heaven Sent

Angels and Ashes

Sins of the Father

Absolution

Lies and Illusions

The Dirty Bitches MC Series

Dirty Bitches MC #1

Dirty Bitches MC #2

Dirty Bitches MC #3

Other Books by Avelyn Paige

Girl in a Country Song

Cassie's Court

About the Authors

Geri Glenn writes alpha males. She is a USA Today Bestselling Author, best known for writing motorcycle romance, including the Kings of Korruption MC series. She lives in the Thousand Islands with her two young girls, one big dog and one terrier that thinks he's a Doberman, a hamster, and two guinea pigs whose names she can never remember.

Before she began writing contemporary romance, Geri worked at several different occupations. She's been a pharmacy assistant, a 911 dispatcher, and a caregiver in a nursing home. She can say without a doubt though, that her favorite job is the one she does now–writing romance that leaves an impact.

Want to talk books? Join Geri's Facebook group to learn about new releases, future series, and to hang out with other readers.

ALSO BY GERI GLENN

The Kings of Korruption MC series.

Ryker

Tease

Daniel

Jase

Reaper

Bosco

Korrupted Novellas:

Corrupted Angels

Reinventing Holly

Other Books by Geri Glenn

Dirty Deeds (Satan's Wrath MC)

Hood Rat